THE CULT CALLED FREEDOM HOUSE

STEPHANIE EVELYN

THE CULT CALLED FREEDOM HOUSE

Edited by Erin Sweet Al-Mehairi
Hook of a Book Media
www.hookofabook.wordpress.com

This book is a work of fiction. Names, characters, places, and incidents either are products of the author's imagination or are used fictitiously. Any resemblance to actual persons, living or dead, events, or locales is entirely coincidental.

Thank you to my mother, Lorraine Ramirez and my father, David Ramirez. Most of all, thank you to my husband, Nicholas Briggs.

You believed in me since the beginning.

FOREWORD

I hate forewords but I will say this. This book is not for the faint of heart.

PREFACE

Everyone but Sophia and Cyrus were going to die. They were goners well before they knew it. Samantha was only fourteen and looking for what every fourteen-year-old looks for— freedom. She wanted to be as far away from her mother as possible, but never this far. It always starts with just one person and one fucked up idea. This is the story about the cult called Freedom House.

CHAPTER ONE

"We need you inside us. It's the only way. You'll live on through us. All of Freedom House will breathe you and reach enlightenment because of you," Cyrus said.

Wearing only a white apron and white panties, Penelope sat next to Cyrus as he spoke to Finn.

"You'll taste so good for our souls," said Penelope.

"You know I'll do anything for Freedom House and for our Journey to Freedom," Finn said, his eyes glazed over with an admiration that no one could snap out of him. It was an anxious, wide-eyed stare full of glee; twinkling stars against a dark sky where blackholes lurked.

Cyrus stared into those twinkling eyes and smiled ever so slightly.

"Penelope, get your cutlery. We will need Finn served to Freedom House for dinner," Cyrus said.

"Sounds delicious," said Penelope.

"Cyrus, I just want to say thank you for letting me be part of something so important. I was never noticed on the outside, but here, I'm someone with meaning," Finn said.

"My dear Finn, your importance is going to live on forever," Cyrus said. "Our pain meditations have prepared you for this moment. The pain you endure today is getting us all closer to enlightenment."

Penelope walked back into Cyrus' room and stood at the doorway entrance, her lanky arms at her side with her long fingers gripping a knife. The tip of her tongue stuck out just enough to hug her bottom lip, caressing it with excitement.

"Lie down and relax Finn," Cyrus said. "You will now be set free. We will see you again once we complete our Journey to Freedom and are set free too."

Finn lay down on the long rug that led from the entrance way to where he and Cyrus sat. Cyrus sat in a cross-legged position in a meditative posture, as he watched Finn.

"Penelope, he's all yours."

Barefoot, Penelope skipped down the long rug to Cyrus and Finn. With her boney, pale legs, she straddled Finn, moved her face down to his and licked his cheek. She lifted herself back up and brought the knife up to his neck. Finn closed his eyes as Cyrus sat and watched.

CHAPTER TWO

Samantha stared out at the crashing waves. She often cut school to watch the surfers at West Cliff conquer the monstrous waters that were the backdrop to Santa Cruz. California was thought to breed golden-haired, bronzed-skin babes who had the summer of their lives, driving with the windows down and blasting Bob Marley. Samantha Watson was not this summer fox. She was raised in the underbelly of Santa Cruz. The one that created the accidents of the city. Santa Cruz was also known for the Pacific Avenue runaways, rejects, drug addicts, and the real punk rockers who lived so far to the edge of society that any slight push might send them off into the depths of hell.

The sun-streaked images of cute kids in Ray-Bans and swimsuits at the beach were mainly reserved for tourists and the UC Santa Cruz college students who piled into the city each year. Yet the

natives of Santa Cruz, they were different. Not quite your Teen Magazine centerfolds.

Samantha climbed down the hill toward the ocean. She sat on a rock with her brown satchel strapped around her body. It hung to the left and displayed her many collections of buttons. *Read a fucking book. Sex Pistols. Misfits. The Clash. Namaste. Free. I hate Santa Cruz.* She unbuckled the satchel straps and opened her bag, grabbing a lime green transparent lighter and a Marlboro Red.

She smoked her first cigarette when she was eight. It was a normal boring Saturday. Her mom, Darleen, had already drank her two coffee mugs of vodka cran and was sloshed by 10:30 a.m. Darleen left her cigarettes on the living room coffee (vodka) table and proceeded to use the bathroom, but didn't come back out for another hour. Samantha was watching one of the six movies she owned: *The Lost Boys.* The opening scene of the Santa Cruz boardwalk played behind The Doors' People are Strange, a perfect backdrop for the blood sucking mayhem that lay ahead. Samantha liked the idea of the boardwalk pariahs leading the underground madness of Santa Cruz, and the whole vampire thing was a nice cherry on top.

She sat back on the stained, faded orange and white couch. Her mother's cigarettes blocked the bottom of the T.V. so she leaned over to move the Marlboro Red box, and once she picked them up, her inner pariah was awakened. *The Lost Boys* and Marlboro Reds were one of the best Saturday morning choices she had ever made. The light headedness and relaxed warmth she felt inside her body is what kept her going back from that day forward. The lost boys did what they wanted, when they wanted, and people were afraid of them. It was not just about being afraid of what they might do. It was also that, as vampires, nothing preyed on them and that's what made them so free. Samantha wanted nothing more but to feel that way; to live that way.

CHAPTER THREE

He sat in his office staring at the stacks of files across his desk. The bags under his eyes depicted a man that hadn't had a good night's sleep in years and the hardened wrinkles on his face were traces of the past haunting him. He sat back in his brown leather chair and loosened his tie around his neck, unbuttoning the top button of his white shirt. He grabbed a file off his desk and a white rectangular sticker in the upper left corner read: Boulder Creek, Case #28968. He heard a knock on his office door and threw the file back onto his desk.

"Come in," he said.

In walked Officer Sophia Rey. "Evening Detective Salvino. You wanted to see me?"

"Please have a seat," Detective Salvino said.

"Officer Rey, I'm sorry to hear about what happened to your father. If you need to take some time off that won't be a problem."

"Thank you, sir," she said. "I'd rather not though." She held back the tears behind her stern eyes and swallowed the knot down into her throat.

The emptiness of losing someone was not new to her. A piece of her heart taken and never replaced was too familiar a feeling and now her heart was being chopped at again. At least her father died in a dignified way, not like her little sister Charlotte.

Officer Rey had shoulder-length, dark brown hair pulled back into a bun and dark, almond-shaped eyes, with a slender face accentuating her sharp facial features. She wore little make-up but her natural look was a delicate beauty, the type that can't go unnoticed. Her hardened eyes collided with her delicateness.

"Sophia, I think it might be a good idea," Detective Salvino said. "What happened to Charlotte was not your fault. You were just a kid."

Officer Rey broke eye contact with the detective and she stared down at his desk. Thoughts raced through her mind as she decided what to say next. She moved her eyes back to his.

"Sir, I'm not taking time off."

"Sophia. You can search your entire life for what happened and never get one step closer to the truth. Do you really want to live your life that way?"

"I can also search my entire life and find out something, anything, about what happened to her."

Detective Salvino nodded his head and gave her a gentle smile.

"Well, if you need anything, I'll be here."

Sophia stood up and walked to the door.

"Detective, what about you? The Boulder Creek case is over, and it's been over for some time," she said, moving her eyes down to the file on his desk.

"Exactly my point, officer. Take it from someone who knows."

CHAPTER FOUR

When Samantha wasn't at the beach cutting school, she was cutting school in downtown Santa Cruz on Pacific Avenue with the punk rockers, runaways, and the born and bred natives who shared her same broken home, shit life. She had just turned fourteen that summer and was planning to leave school behind and live the runaway life. She wouldn't be missing anything by leaving her mom and she knew she wouldn't be missed either. All her mother cared about was vodka and bringing home lazy, booze smelling pervs, and for some reason, her mother lived for the abuse.

"What do you think Sam?" Slim Steve nudged her shoulder. He was tall and had short, spikey hair with blue tips. He always wore a jean vest with the sleeves tore off and no shirt underneath. He had a junk habit which made him skinny, so everyone called him Slim

Steve. He was in his early twenties but was beginning to look well over thirty.

"About what?" Samantha asked.

"Haven't you been listening? If you had to choose, you know this is desert island shit, would you choose Sex Pistols or The Clash?"

"Sex Pistols. All the way. Sid Vicious, come on now," Samantha said.

"That's my girl. Sid and Nancy, right?"

Samantha started cutting school last year and met Slim Steve and his punk rock crew when she decided to take a stroll downtown on Pacific Avenue. She discovered the Ramones while hanging around Streetlight Records. Slim Steve was smoking a cigarette out front when Samantha walked out, staring at the back of her new CD *End of the Century*. She stopped out front and sat on the sidewalk concrete, crossed her legs, and began to open it.

He kneeled next to her, cigarette in hand, and blew a cloud of smoke out in front of him. "Heard of Sex Pistols?" he said, with a charming smile, one adorned by two bottom lip piercings, one on each side.

"I've heard of them but never listened to their stuff," Samantha said.

"Ramones is a good pick too. I'm Slim Steve," he said, then turned his cigarette around and held it out to Samantha, a new friendship offering.

She stared at him, then down at the cigarette, the small red burning ball at the tip breathing out curls of smoke. She grabbed the cigarette and took a hit, holding it in long enough for Slim Steve to know that she was not a rookie, regardless of how young she looked. She lifted her head to the sky and blew the smoke out.

"I'm Sam," she said, and they stood up together and walked down Pacific Avenue in combat boots, jean vests, Misfits and The Damned patches, and Slim Steve about a foot taller than her; side by side they walked and became new friends.

CHAPTER FIVE

Officer Sophia Rey had been with the Santa Cruz Police Department for eight years. She moved to Santa Cruz when she was eighteen, attended UCSC, and joined the force at twenty-nine years old. She grew up in San Jose but moved to Santa Cruz. She hadn't been back to San Jose, even though it was only an hour away, for nineteen years. After what happened to her little sister Charlotte, she wanted nothing to do with that place.

She started working with Detective Salvino three years ago and he became a mentor. His twenty years of service made him well respected and he was one of the good detectives— the type that lives to save lives. He was forty-six years old, divorced with no kids, and his life was work. He had black, slick hair that he combed back with gel, hazel eyes, and sported a scruffy beard. The wrinkles around his eyes and mouth only added to his masculinity and good looks. He was tired, mentally and emotionally, but he hardly showed it.

He remembered every single one of his cases and every detail, every suspect's name and especially every victim's name. He was known for saving more people than any other detective over the last twenty years in Santa Cruz County. Even with this track record, he still had failed with the Boulder Creek case and the eighteen victims he failed to save that day. He couldn't forget what happened in Boulder Creek six years ago. He was haunted by it every night. Nine were just kids, and it was his job to help them, but he was too late. He knew it was over and now a part of a dark past that hovered over the city of Santa Cruz, but that didn't matter to him. He thought differently. He obsessed over every detail of that day. Every phone call, every turn, every itch, and every word possibly spoken that surrounded the horrific event.

He obsessed over it because he knew that when others believed something over, it wasn't always. Evil lived on. It might die away in one instance but would always be reborn into another. He knew that. He had to study every detail of Boulder Creek and how he failed it because he knew he would face evil again soon. Rumor was that one male escaped the Boulder Creek Kingdom of Light cult. Late at night, when the world was asleep, this rumor nudged at Detective Salvino's gut, waking him and keeping him awake, to only stare up at his ceiling in the dark all alone.

CHAPTER SIX

Officer Rey sat on the bench in front of the Santa Cruz PD building. The early morning ocean mist floated through the air and filled her nose with the smell of sea salt and fish. She sipped her coffee. Since living in Santa Cruz, she drank her coffee black, and if she could get it darker she would.

Detective Salvino walked out the building and stood next to the bench, pulling out a cigarette and lighting it. He took a hit and they stayed there silently in each other's presence, enjoying the morning fresh air, free of the violence and death for which they were so accustomed.

"Mornin' Officer Rey."

"Good morning," she said, and took another sip of coffee.

"So, are you going to the service? It's in San Jose, isn't it?" Detective Salvino knew she hadn't been back home in years.

"Don't know. I haven't thought about it," she said.

He sat on the bench with her.

"I know it's hard. I wish I could say it's gonna get easier but I'm not going to bullshit you."

Officer Rey looked up from her coffee into his calming eyes, "Thank you."

"Sometimes when the pain is overbearing, we aren't ourselves. You might want to hide from it but later you might regret it and that's something you can't undo."

Officer Rey stared at the yellow flowers that adorned the grass in front of them, and just listened.

"How's your mom?" Detective Salvino asked.

"Don't know. We don't talk much. She blames me for Charlotte."

"Sophia, if you need anything, you know my door is always open," he said.

"I know, detective," she said, and took another drink of her coffee. He stood up and walked back inside. "Thanks again."

Officer Rey had thought about her father's upcoming funeral service. It was almost the only thing she thought about, but she knew she wasn't going back to San Jose. She had last seen her mother five years ago when her parents came to visit her in Santa Cruz. It was, of course, her dad's idea.

She was a daddy's girl. She got her first switchblade when she was seven years old from her dad and he taught her how to use it.

"It's better for you to understand how to handle a knife than to hurt yourself with one," he had said.

He always seemed to know about everything and explain it in such a way that just made sense. He was a police officer and took pride in hard work and dedication.

He would tell Sophia, "When you grow up, you get a job, you work real hard, and you get to live the life you want."

Michael Rey was a police officer for thirty years but before that he almost landed a life in prison. He was raised on welfare and grew up in San Jose, impoverished with a raging alcoholic for a father. The shred of hope he received was not from his parents but instead from his idols on television. He was the only person Sophia knew that was both street smart and book smart. Aside from the alcoholism that ran in his family, he came from a long line of intelligent and eccentric ancestors, which he would use to his advantage later and pass on to Charlotte and Sophia.

It wasn't until his twenties when he started to read books about the birth of the universe and the science of Man. Once he discovered Carl Sagan and Shakespeare, his life went onto a very different trajectory than the statistics would predict. He inhaled every bit of knowledge he could get his hands on and was part of the generation who ordered full Encyclopedia sets by landline phone. Working hard, reading, and being a good father were what he lived for.

Michael's father was a professional boxer who never made it big. He was not a happy alcoholic either. Michael's childhood memories were made of fist fights and the smell of whiskey and slur of cuss words. The intelligence gene came from his dad's side but so did the addictive one. A constant internal battle between logic and pleasure.

When Sophia's mother got pregnant with Sophia, Michael made it a point to do everything opposite his father. He knew the darkness of addiction was always lurking deep in the shadows, ready to swallow him up at the perfect opportunity. And there are many perfect opportunities. Addiction makes friends with mental weakness and promises an instant fix for it, but it's never enough. It was never enough for Sophia's grandfather.

Michael embraced his intelligent gene and told the addictive one to fuck off. When she was growing up, he spent most of his free time with Sophia. He taught her how to fix things and build things. He taught her about the musical geniuses of every era. He was involved in her hobbies and school activities. And above all, he never drank, not even on holidays. When Charlotte was born, he made sure to never show his favorite, but they all knew. Sophia had a special place in his heart. Charlotte was closer to her mother, Meredith.

Meredith's childhood was very different than Michael's and so was her relationship with Sophia. It would later become a relationship stained with resentment, blame, and hate. And when Michael and Meredith visited Sophia in Santa Cruz five years ago, it didn't get any better and she and her mother hadn't spoken since. Now, Sophia's sister and father were dead, and she knew she would have to speak to her mother.

CHAPTER SEVEN

Samantha walked into the kitchen and stared at the pile of dirty dishes that called the sink home for the past two weeks. Trails of black ants marched around dirty plates and crawled across the counter. The stove was hardly used, and crusty grime had built up around the burners.

She opened the refrigerator with high hopes and used her imagination to think about if it was clean inside and filled with a functional family's supply of bright red strawberries, juicy green grapes, fresh milk, and a carton of eggs. When she swung the refrigerator door open, her hope died from the stench of rotting lunch meat and moldy cheese. There was one carton of milk, but she knew better than to stick her nose into the top. She was used to that sour dairy smell that hits your throat and moves into your stomach, poking at it and instigating reflux.

There was nothing else except two forties of Old English and cranberry juice. She had planned to go to class today but she was hungry and figured Slim Steve might be able to help.

She walked through the living room to the front door of the apartment and turned around to look at her mom. She was passed out on the couch in underwear and some guy's large, black shirt. A lit cigarette hung from her right hand and was about to fall onto the carpet. Samantha walked over and grabbed the cigarette out of her mom's hand and stuck it in her own mouth.

Darleen opened her eyes and wiped the drool that was hanging down the side of her face.

"Samantha? Where are you going?"

"To school," she said, and took a drag of the cigarette.

"What the fuck is that? Give me my cigarette," she said, already slurring and it wasn't even nine o' clock yet.

"We have no food," Samantha said.

"You think I can't fuckin see. Bobby's pickin' some up later," she said. Maybe Bobby was the guy's shirt she was wearing, maybe not.

"Your school called. You haven't been showing up."

"Since when do you care? You don't even buy food for the house, but you have plenty of vodka," Samantha said, holding the front door open.

"What the fuck did you say you little bitch?" Darleen grabbed the cigarette ashtray from the coffee table and without hesitating threw it at Samantha. She had the aim and distance of a drunk, lazy slob. It hit the carpet a couple feet away from Samantha's feet. Samantha looked down at the ashtray and walked out the door, slamming it behind her.

She found Slim Steve at the Bonesio Liquor Store at the end of Pacific Avenue. He wore gray fingerless gloves and smoked a cigarette.

"Mornin' sunshine," Slim Steve said.

"Hey," Samantha said, but didn't crack a smile.

"You okay?" Slim Steve asked.

"I'll be alright," Samantha said, then took a cigarette out of her satchel, and when Slim Steve took his lighter out, she lit it and he held his hand around the flame, leaning in toward her.

"Thanks," she said.

"I almost forgot. I got you an egg McMuffin," Slim Steve said, taking his backpack off and unzipping it, handing her the greasy sandwich.

"I told you I was going to class today, not coming here, so why did you get this for me?" Samantha held it in her hand and stared at him.

"I know but I collected some cash this morning and figured I might see you anyway and you might be hungry."

Samantha looked at him, right in his eyes. "Thanks, Steve."

"Forget about it," he said, as he scratched his forearm. "I got somewhere to be. I won't be long, just like ten minutes. Will you wait up for me?" he said.

"Can I just come with you?"

"I don't think that's a good idea, Sam."

"Why not?" Samantha asked.

"I'll only be like ten minutes. I promise."

"Alright," Samantha sat on the curb and unwrapped her breakfast sandwich. She watched Slim Steve walk down a residential street, away from downtown. She looked at her sandwich and scarfed it down.

CHAPTER EIGHT

"One of our new members wants to leave. She wants to go back home," Jonas said, sitting on the floor with Cyrus.

Cyrus' long, straight hair hung down the left and right sides of his chest.

"That's not a possibility at Freedom House. We can't have someone leaving and jeopardizing our Journey to Freedom," said Cyrus.

"This I know. I can take care of it," Jonas said.

"Please do and do so quietly. We can't distract the others."

"Of course," said Jonas, and he got up to leave Cyrus' room.

"Jonas," Cyrus said, still sitting on the floor.

Jonas turned around and stood at the doorway.

"All our small problems need to go to the Red Room. Understand?"

"I understand Cyrus," said Jonas and he walked out.

Penelope had been sitting in the room, watching them and listening to their conversation.

"Penelope, come over to me," said Cyrus.

Staying on the floor, Penelope switched her seated position and got on her hands and knees. She crawled in her white apron and underwear over to Cyrus then sat on her knees.

"Join Jonas and assist him in the Red Room. He doesn't have a key to that room yet."

She reached her hand into the left pocket of her apron and moved the key between her fingers.

"It needs to happen right now," said Cyrus.

"Anything for you Cyrus. How do you want it done?"

"When someone wants to leave Freedom House, it means they didn't belong here in the first place. We don't consume those types of people into our bodies. They deserve to be taught a lesson in conviction."

"Agreed. They are brought to us for a reason. We owe it to them to teach them," said Penelope.

Cyrus reached both his hands out and put them around Penelope's face, cupping her cheeks. He leaned in and kissed her forehead.

"And you were also brought to me for a reason Penelope. You understand our journey. Now help us get closer to it."

Penelope stood up and skipped out of the room.

CHAPTER NINE

Sophia's police car was parked at the Santa Cruz Metro Station, which landmarked the center of downtown Santa Cruz. She sat in the car and scanned the many characters walking past as she sipped her coffee. UCSC students walked by in small groups and from places that smelled of southern California, with designer shoes and wallets full of cash that their parents sent every month.

Metro Station was also the hub for the homeless and small-time drug dealers. The tourists don't always know this, but Santa Cruz has a meth problem. And every year, the college students become a target for business. The dealers can smell it. They come to college mainly to party, score, get laid, and if they have time, maybe go to class.

Something caught Sophia's attention. A man wearing a black-hooded sweater and blue jeans was standing near the Metro entrance doors and facing out toward Pacific Avenue. He stood with a comfortable ease like it was where he was supposed to be each day.

A tall, skinny man approached him. The guy looked to be about thirty years old and had spiky hair with a jean vest. The vest was covered in patches with band names and silver studs. He stood next to the man in the hooded sweater and looked out toward the street, lips moving in conversation but not facing the man. The man's lips moved, and he nodded his head to the punk rock guy.

The punk rocker walked away and went around the Metro Station building. Sophia just watched and sipped her coffee again. A few minutes later, the man in the hooded sweater followed and disappeared behind the building. Sophia got out of the car and walked over to the entrance. She peeked around the building wall and saw the two, side-by-side. The dealer had a small, black balloon tied up.

"Hi boys. How's it going?" Officer Rey said after turning the corner to face their direction.

The dealer did not hesitate to immediately begin running the opposite direction. He pushed the punk rocker out of his way and ran with full speed around the backside of the Metro Station.

"Stop right there!" Officer Rey chased after him.

The punk rocker watched Sophia run around the backside of the building. He looked down at the ground and right next to his combat boot was the black balloon filled with smack goodness. He bent over, picked it up, put it into his pocket, and walked down the street to Cheddar Boy's house.

CHAPTER TEN

"What's your name?" Sophia was driving back to the police department.

"Fuck off," the dealer was in the back of the car with a bloody nose and a pissed off look on his face as he stared out the window.

"Classy," Officer Rey looked at him in her rearview.

She had chased this fast fuck all the way down to Mission Street. She jumped for his legs and slammed him to the ground and he still tried to kick her off. She only had to punch him once for him to throw in the towel. And now here they were. She drove with strands of hair pulled out of her bun and Mr. Track Runner had a bloody nose.

"Who you working for?" Officer Rey asked with a calmness in her voice.

"I'm not telling you shit lady."

"Your loyalty is admirable but your boss doesn't care about you," she said.

"You have no idea what you're talking about," he said.

They pulled up to the station and she opened the back door, pulling him out of the car.

"You're pretty hot for a cop. You should consider doing undercover prostitute shit." He laughed.

Sophia ignored his comments and walked him into the station.

Slim Steve didn't need to knock.

Everyone just let themselves in and that was always okay with Cheddar Boy. There wasn't anything of value in that house anyways except for the value that was being injected there. Crack houses were only good for one thing, but it was the closest thing to a home that Slim Steve had.

The house once belonged to Cheddar Boy's grandfather and he passed it on to Cheddar's mom. It was paid off and was once a livable family home. Cheddar's mom trashed it and let anyone who had two legs crash there. It didn't take long for the place to become a shelter for meth addicts and head nodders.

It was a single-story house with a front yard full of dead grass and tall weeds, and a shopping cart in the center of them. The screen door was torn, and the mesh hung over on its side. Slim Steve opened the door and walked in. It was dark and musty. The living room window, which at one time had beautiful plum curtains, was now adorned with a brown blanket that stunk like piss and vomit. There was one couch against the wall, but it was torn, and cotton bulged out, spilling onto the floor. The carpet was stained with God knows what and crust had built-up on the carpet hairs.

The walls were dirty with brown and yellow splotches and there were piles of trash, clothes, blankets, and boxes across the floor. A person had to focus in on a pile to then determine what was in it. A toothbrush here, spoon there, an empty bag of Oreos, maybe even a used condom.

Slim Steve sat on the couch next to Cheddar Boy.

"Whassup Cheddar. Where's Benny?" he said, holding his fist out, and Cheddar returned the gesture. Benjamin Miles Wilson was Cheddar's brother.

"I don't know. He's on a whole other level. Some shit about finding enlightenment and freedom. Bullshit. He'll be back. You score today?" Cheddar had thick, curly brown hair that went right past his chin, but he always pulled it back into a ponytail. His was pale and had freckles on his face and arms.

"You know it," Slim Steve said, and took the balloon out of his pocket.

Slim Steve tied his arm with a belt that was on the floor and got to work. Cheddar too. They laid back against the couch and gradual relaxation moved from the tops of their heads down their faces, through their chests, caressed their groins, and tickled their toes. Their eyelids fell toward the bottom lid, a weight not on their shoulders but instead which massaged their heads; far more desirable. They sat there in silence for a couple of hours. Slim Steve forgot about Samantha and everything else.

CHAPTER ELEVEN

Samantha sat on the curb and played with her lighter. She had been waiting for twenty minutes now, so she took out another cigarette. As she was lighting it, she heard shouting. She turned to look down Pacific Ave. and some man in a black sweater was running in her direction. He turned his head to look behind him and kept alternating between looking ahead and looking behind. He ran past Samantha and she watched him run down the block.

A female police officer was not far behind him and ran past Samantha a few seconds later. Samantha thought for a moment that the guy looked familiar, but she wasn't sure. She stood up and was about to start walking,

"Did you see that shit?" A guy walked up next to her. He had brown flowing pants and a tight, white shirt that showcased his toned muscles. He wore a hiking backpack, the type that could carry more than fifty pounds.

"Pretty crazy but not surprised," Samantha said.

"Can I bum one?" he asked.

"Sure," she said, and handed him a cigarette, pulling her lighter out.

"Thanks. I'm Miles," he said, holding his hand out.

"Samantha," she said.

"So, where you headed with that backpack," Samantha asked with a chuckle.

"Who wants to know?"

"I won't tell. Pinky promise," said Samantha.

"I'm doing a food and water run," he said.

"Did I miss the memo that it was the zombie apocalypse?" she asked, with another chuckle.

He laughed and his charming smile never ceased, "Funny. I live in a commune. I used to live down here in this dump. The streets just eat people alive. It'll swallow you whole down here and then you'll disappear. My brother lives around here, but I don't want anything to do with him."

"It's pretty shitty, for sure. So, how many people live in this commune?"

"There's about fifty of us. Like a big family. Something I've never had before."

"Sounds cool. Where's it at?"

"Well, if I told you that I'd have to kill you," he said and started to laugh. Samantha laughed too.

"We're up 1 North, about twenty minutes from here."

They walked slowly down Pacific Ave.

"Can I come with you," she asked.

"We just met— what are you like twelve years old?"

"I'm fourteen and I'm planning on running away anyways. So, I'll be on the streets. You said it yourself, this place eats people alive and they disappear. I'd still rather be on the streets than living at home. But what are the odds that you would ask me for a cigarette?"

Miles looked at her and his smile faded for a moment, "You're serious?"

"Please," Samantha said, her eyes desperate.

He knew the commune was open to new members, and he knew the commune accepted underaged kids, but he also knew there were things there that, although he could handle them, Samantha probably couldn't. She seemed like a nice girl who had lost her way and he didn't want to lead her somewhere she could get more lost, but he knew what the streets had done to his brother Cheddar Boy. So, he took a gamble.

"Under one condition," he said.

"Anything."

"You have to throw away your cigarettes. And I never bummed one off you, got it?"

Placing her cigarettes on the curb, they walked off Pacific Avenue.

CHAPTER TWELVE

Sophia sat in the police car at the station. She picked up her phone and dialed. It rang, and rang, and rang. Someone picked up on the other line but said nothing, just silence.

"Mom?"

Silence.

"It's me, Sophia."

In a low soft voice her mother said, "I know who it is."

"Mom, how are you doing?"

"How do you think? I lost my little girl and now my husband. The two most important people in my life have been taken."

Sophia's heart sank and she held back tears and anger.

"I know it's not easy, especially with the service coming up. I was wondering if—"

"Sophia, don't bother. I haven't seen you in years and I don't want your father's service to be dampened in any way. I just want peace."

A tear rolled down Sophia's cheek for her father's sake, but her heart raced with anger that boiled inside for her mother's sake.

"Right," Sophia said.

"I'm not sure what the point of this call was for," her mother said.

"He was my father. And she was my sister." Sophia hung up the phone and pushed her face into the steering wheel.

Slim Steve opened his eyes and even the dark room hurt his head. He reached into his pocket and pulled out the balloon, but it was empty. He ripped the balloon and flattened it out for anything but there was nothing left. Cheddar was still passed out on the couch, mouth wide open and spit rolling down his mouth.

Slim Steve didn't know what time it was. He walked over to the kitchen, if you could even call it that. It was just another storage room for trash and miscellaneous items that junkies and meth heads left behind. He looked around for something to use as a cup to get some water. He could hardly swallow. His throat was so dry that if he swallowed, he'd choke on his own uvula. He searched the kitchen and saw an Egg McMuffin wrapper in the sink.

The thought of Samantha pierced his brain, like a deep knife shoved in and turned violently. Before running out of the house, he turned the faucet on, shoved his head under it, and sucked the water into his mouth. Then he left and booked it down Pacific Ave. He went to the liquor store where he had given her the breakfast sandwich hours earlier, but he was too late. There was no sign of Samantha. Slim Steve turned around and went back to Cheddar Boy's house.

CHAPTER THIRTEEN

His real name was Benjamin Wilson, but he disowned Benjamin. Miles was a name given to him by the commune, even though it was his true middle name. When he met Samantha on Pacific Ave. that day, they became friends, even though he was six years older than her at twenty.

Formerly going by Benny, Miles was from Los Angeles and came to Santa Cruz when he was eighteen years old to attend University of California, Santa Cruz. He was going to be a Psychology major but dropped out at the end of his freshman year. His parents wanted him to attend a four year university and that was the only one he got into. Like his brother, he wanted to attend a city college in L.A., but they didn't support that idea. His brother Eric, later to be called Cheddar, dropped out quickly and followed his brother to Santa Cruz because he heard he could make a living slanging drugs to the locals.

Los Angeles was a city that never slept and where every scene had a place: punk rockers, hipsters, artists, musicians, and the lists and sublists go on forever, just like the city life— awake all day and all night. Santa Cruz was different and for someone who came from a big city, the boredom, and single, solitary downtown street of Pacific Avenue could drive anyone to insanity. It even drove the locals into a certain state of crazy; a crazy that smelled of sea salt air, small town meth addicts, unwashed clumped hair, and a slight stench of patchouli. A Santa Cruz crazy. *Keep Santa Cruz weird. Should have been: Stay in Santa Cruz and you'll go crazy.*

Benny had attended most of his first year at UCSC but quickly learned how lonely Santa Cruz could get. The same three good restaurants, the same concerts at The Catalyst (if you can even call them concerts), the same bar with a pool table, and the damn Surf's Up bar. Surf's Up was the only legitimate club in Santa Cruz. The first floor was quiet and reserved for Literature majors who wanted to discuss Bronte, Homer, and Toni Morrison on a Saturday night. The upstairs was for everyone else. It was loud and shit music was always playing the Top Hits on the radio, more like Top Shits. Everyone had to shout to talk, it was elbow to elbow, and felt like a sauna the moment you walked in, but there was a bar and if you were underage you could just get someone to buy you a drink.

Surf's Up got old real fast. Benny had been used to the Los Angeles night scene which meant you could go to different spots for weeks at a time before hitting up the same spot again. You felt like jazz? There was a place in L.A. for that. Blues? That too. Punk Rock? Classic Rock? Music festival? Pool billiards? There were tons. He began to feel confined and couldn't breathe in Santa Cruz. He wanted to be free again, but his parents were threatening to throw him out if he left school to go back to L.A. They were paying his way through college and putting money into his bank account each month, but only as long as he attended UCSC.

Benny had stopped going to some of his classes to go surfing, probably the only bright light that existed in Santa Cruz. The one thing the town had going for it was the ocean. When loneliness sets in, and internal monsters come out, the ocean always seems to console. There's something about its violent waves, its threatening nature combined with its vast beauty, that liberates the soul just from staring at it. That's what Benny loved about surfing.

That's where he first met them. They called themselves Freedom House and their leader was a man named Cyrus. Benny had just gotten back onto shore from surfing and saw around fifteen people sitting in a circle with one man standing in the center. They were meditating and all dressed similar except for the man standing in the middle of the circle. They all wore brown flowing pants and the males wore white shirts and the females had on bikini tops. The man in the center wore an elaborate vest with no shirt underneath. The vest was white with a detailed black embroidered design. He had long, golden brown hair that blew in the wind, soft as silk on your skin. They were chanting something, and Benny was intrigued. He stared from afar.

The man caught his stare and whispered something to one of the girls. She got up and walked over to Benny. She stood in front of Benny and didn't say anything. She stared into his eyes with her piercing blue ones. A stranger digging into the depths of his soul with just a stare.

"How's it going?" Benny asked, with a slight uncomfortable chuckle.

"It's going perfect. Cyrus saw you staring at us. He is inviting you to come over and meditate with us," said the girl.

"I was staring because there aren't too many people that know about this beach. You have a pretty large group there."

"So, are you going to join us?"

Benny looked down at the wetsuit he had on.

"I don't think it's a good idea. I'm all wet and—"

"We don't mind. We'd love to have you join us. You'll really like Cyrus and the rest of Freedom House," she said.

"Freedom House?" he said.

"Yes. Have you ever experienced real freedom? If you come with us, we can promise you a life of true freedom," she said.

Benny looked back at the group sitting on the sand and their leader Cyrus caught his eyes and gave him a gentle smile. Benny thought about his parents and school. He thought about how he just wanted to be on his own but didn't have the means to live on his own.

The girl grabbed his hand, smiled at him, and began to walk to the circle, gently pulling Benny along with her. He followed.

"Can I get your name?" Benny asked.

"I'm Penelope."

That's the day Benny joined Freedom House and that's the day he stopped going by Benny and started to go by Miles.

CHAPTER FOURTEEN

Nestled in the depths of the woods, the people living at Freedom House had everything they ever needed: food, water, and a community where love, peace, and freedom were the purpose of living and the center of their lives. At least, that's how it started out.

Miles brought Samantha to the house and for the first time in her life she felt safe. The entrance was inviting in a way that was unexplainable, but it pulled her toward it, almost like a force. She couldn't turn away. There was a white picket fence surrounding the house and green vine tendrils wrapped and twisted around the fence, keeping it in its grip and never letting go. Behind the fence, lay a small garden with tomatoes, squash, carrots, and herbs.

The house was single story and the dark grey paint was free of cracks and stains. There was a wooden sign nailed above the door, and in white cursive lettering it read: Freedom House. A large porch wrapped around and was home to a swinging bench and colorful pillows which lay along the porch, waiting for bodies to occupy them.

They walked through the garden and down a small stone path to the porch, sharp sun rays lit up the porch stairs.

"There's no other place like this," Samantha said.

"It's nice out here. Better than that downtown dump," Miles said.

Samantha stared down at the porch steps and touched the wooden railing leading onto the porch.

Miles walked up the steps and stood at the top step, turning around to face Samantha. He held his hand out and said,

"Aren't you coming?"

Samantha didn't say anything. She walked up the steps and onto the porch. She looked at the wooden panels on the floor. The worn-out panels told a story of community, love, and long nights spent there. There was a light brown swinging bench with a teal blanket thrown across. Miles sat on the bench.

"Have a seat," he tapped the open space next to him.

Samantha sat down. Miles began swinging the bench in a slow and soothing motion, repetitive and melodic.

"I can't believe this place exists here," Samantha said.

"Sometimes you have to leave what you know to find things you never knew about," said Miles.

Samantha looked out, past the porch stairs, through the garden full of greens, reds, and oranges, and out to the large open meadow. The meadow stretched across the front of Freedom House. There were no other houses in sight. No other signs of life except for the distant sounds of birds in the mornings and wolves at night. A reminder that the comfort of daylight will always disappear into the unknown darkness of the night.

The meadow eventually reached the edge of the woods. The crowded redwood trees stood tall, always watching Freedom House. Day and night, the darkness loomed around, behind, and in between the redwoods. The trees kept it contained.

The swing moved forward and back, forward and back, and Miles turned watching Samantha.

"Welcome to Freedom House."

CHAPTER FIFTEEN

Sophia went back to San Jose the day before her father's service. It was a sunny Saturday afternoon as she drove over the winding, narrow turns of Highway 17. Every year, at least one person died on 17. She remembered an accident that happened two years before when she was the first officer at the scene.

It was one of those gloomy days where the sky overwhelmed the world below with gray clouds and strong, heavy winds. The wind would push against cars as they raced along the 17, fighting against them and hoping to win by flipping them over. Sophia remembered when she got the call about the accident, she had turned her wipers on at the highest speed and still couldn't see in front of her. The road was an explosion of water that sprayed out in all directions and blocked her view. She knew each second wasted having to drive slower meant death was getting closer. It was a race between her and that darkness. It always was.

Every detail, every smell, every part of that accident was burned into her brain. It was an old Honda Civic that had spun out of control, a consequence of combining speed with wet pavement. Upon spinning out, the Honda ended up facing the wrong way and the car directly behind slammed into it, causing a three-car pile-up. Each car slammed into the car in front of it, hitting the Honda each time with a little more force.

Sophia had to drive the shoulder since the two lanes were dead stop. When she got to the scene and ran up to the accident, she could see the disaster behind the falling rain and heavy fog.

Sophia ran to the Honda. Its front was crushed all the way into the start of the back seat. She grabbed her flashlight and rain hit her face; water dripped down her cheeks and slid into the crease of her lips. Fog creeped between the crushed car and the rain slammed down onto the shattered windshield. Sophia shone her flashlight through a sliver of space created by the jagged broken window. She could make out shards of glass, blood dripping down pieces of sharp metal, and long dark hair.

She turned the light at a different angle, and she shouted, "Can you hear me? I'm here to help. I'm Officer Rey."

There was no movement except the rain pouring down. Sophia maneuvered her arm through the driver's side shattered window. She reached her hand toward the girl in the driver's seat to check for a pulse. The girl's head was bent forward, and her chin was pushed against her neck. Officer Rey placed her two fingers on the side of the girl's neck the best she could, but instead of a pulse, Sophia Rey just felt the warm and wet blood that seeped out from somewhere.

Sophia snapped out of this horrible memory when a red Harley zoomed by her car and moved in front of her, growling at her to wake up. She realized then that the curved highway in front of her was completely blurred out as she thought about that girl from two years ago. She wondered how she didn't get in an accident when her focus left the present and transported to the past.

It wasn't until she pulled into the church parking lot in San Jose that she realized how long she had been daydreaming about her nightmares. She turned her car off and looked up at the overpowering church that towered over her with its intricate carvings and gold trim, crying out for every lost soul that's ever come into contact with it. She still couldn't believe that she'd be saying goodbye to her father forever.

CHAPTER SIXTEEN

Miles held Samantha's hand as they walked into Freedom House for her first time. He opened the front door and led Samantha inside, a comforting smell hitting her nose. The scent of fresh bread baking, rising with a warm, fluffy center and golden crisp outer shell, warmed her body. For the first time in her life, she wasn't suffocated by the smell of cigarettes.

There were people everywhere. Some were cleaning, and some were leading meditation sessions, others were painting. Soft, content smiles floated in the air like they had a mind of their own. Everyone who walked past her had the same bright-eyed look. The smell of basil and fresh bread tugged at her. They walked through the living room, past a few people on the floor in cross-legged positions, and into the kitchen. A young woman was chopping basil on the center marble island. With the swift chopping skills of an expert chef, she looked up to see who was approaching and continued to chop. She had short, pixie, blonde hair, small gem earrings running down her ears one after another, and those bright, blue eyes. She was so thin that it was difficult not to look at her bones sticking out in odd places and she wore an apron with only panties underneath.

"Hello Miles. Who's your guest?" she asked, still chopping the basil but staring at Miles.

"This is Samantha. Well, that's her name from the outside. Samantha this is—"

"I'm Penelope. I'm the Freedom House chef. You are free to eat whatever you find here but I am the only person allowed to cook in the kitchen unless I need help."

Samantha nodded her head. "Thank you so much. I can't thank Miles enough for bringing me here."

Penelope looked into Samantha's eyes. Moving her hand over her mouth, Samantha gasped.

"Your hand is bleeding," Samantha said.

Without flinching, Penelope said, "Oh shame on me. Sometimes I get knife happy when I cook."

She brought her left hand up to her mouth and sucked the blood off her index finger. She used her right hand to squeeze the cut to force more blood out, and then sucked it again. Then, she went back to chopping. Samantha tried not stare in shock.

"Do you need anything for it?" Miles asked.

"It's a small scratch and I'm a big girl," Penelope said. I'll see you around, Samantha. Enjoy your tour."

"Thank you," Samantha said. "I look forward to it."

A backdoor connected the kitchen to the backyard. It was spacious and spanned two acres out. To the left was a small fenced off area with chickens, pigs, and two white peacocks. In the middle was a walking path adorned by rows of lush bushes and flowers. Benches lined the path and a cement, two-tier water fountain was met at the end. To the right was a stone path leading to a koi pond. Underneath the dark blue water, colors of orange, black, and white swam gracefully in spiral motions. Behind the pond was the entrance to another small house. A dark red curtain hung down the doorway.

"This is Freedom Park," Miles said.

"It's just perfect," Samantha said, her head moving from left to middle, then to the right, as she absorbed what she had never seen before and now was seeing for the first time in her life.

"It's yours Samantha. It's all of ours," he said.

"Wow, cool," she said. "This is all so, crazy. But in a good way."

"I always wish someone would've taken a chance on me sooner. If people never gave others a chance, the world would be worse off than it already is. It's up to us to create our own freedom, otherwise we'll die trapped in someone else's. Now it's time to meet Cyrus. He created Freedom House," Miles said. He grabbed her hand and started down the stone path, toward the koi pond.

CHAPTER SEVENTEEN

Sophia stood on the sidewalk and her head tilted all the way up. At the top of the church, the sharp tip of the cross pointed above the white marshmallow clouds.

They never had any type of service for her sister Charlotte. Her mother and father believed that it would mean their surrender. When hope is surrendered, it makes way for a dark reality— the truth.

A breeze brushed Sophia's face after she pulled open the heavy church door and for a second, she thought she heard a whisper so low in her ear that it could have been someone mouthing her name with their lips. The brightness from outside said goodbye as the door swung closed, pushing the light away and leaving Sophia in silence, accompanied by rows of empty pews.

Trying to pierce through the sky, the church ceiling reached high above her head. She stared down the aisle, and in the distance saw his casket. A deep red oak with gold trim as simple and modest as her father but engrained with wisdom and dignity. The thick blue rug pressed against her feet as she walked with the pace of never wanting to get to the end but being forced to. She treated each step as a moment to be shared one last time with her father. She was always a daddy's girl. Memories of her childhood walked her down the aisle toward the casket.

She remembered when she was a little girl. At age five she had quite the collection of stuffed animals, taking up half her entire bed and each one had their particular place in her bedroom. For her fifth birthday, her parents gave her a white and purple tea set. Butterflies flew across the teacups and delicate flowers grew along the small plates. In the corner of her bedroom, two large windows breathed sunlight onto her pink round table for tea parties. Sophia brought chairs in and arranged her stuffed animals around the table. A white rabbit, a small brown teddy bear, a white teddy bear with a red nose, a giraffe, and a Dalmatian dog.

Her mother didn't enjoy playtime. Grasping for imagination is a tragedy that all adults endure but there are special ones that push themselves hard enough to reach the edge of where a child's imagination only just begins. Sophia's father always reached the edge and stayed as long as he could.

Coming home from a long day's work, there was never a hesitation in his mind. With the limited time given in a day, he always made time for Sophia and he thought about it as her making time for him. Traditional work hours didn't exist in his world and every time he stepped foot out of that house, he was putting himself in danger to help others. He always knew he wanted to be a cop. Not the shit kind. Not the kind who live their lives fueled on racism and hate. He wanted to be the best damn cop he could ever be, and he showed that every day.

Michael Rey was largely built. Along his arms, neck, and chest were the permanent markings of a rough childhood: tattoos that told a story of dark and deadly street corners and unsupervised and dirty living rooms where anything could be consumed. A lost boy who would later be found. He had dark black hair and a mustache that was kept cleaned up. He was the kind of person who was scary, not afraid of anything, but had a softness for the profound things in life. Things that most other people are oblivious to or take for granted. He retold stories about Atticus Finch and Jake LaMotta; retelling their moments of pain and triumph. Sophia didn't understand it all until she was older, but it forever set her up to be special like him.

She hadn't noticed, but her eyes filled heavily with tears as she walked toward the casket. The peak of his nose and the tip of his chin came into view first. He came dressed to the occasion as he always did, looking damn good and dignified. Hair slicked back, shiny and sleek, and a black suit and black tie against a white, button up shirt. She stopped at the casket and gripped the edges with her fingers and then fell to her knees, her arms still up and her hands still holding onto the edge of the casket. Echoed sounds of her sobs vibrated against the church walls and floated up to the very top of the church ceiling.

CHAPTER EIGHTEEN

Miles led her into the room behind the koi pond. Tea light candles trailed along the perimeter of each wall and provided the only light around them. There was a long, dark red carpet that started at the doorway and ran all the way down to a man who sat crossed legged on the floor, tapestries and candles shining behind him, creating a dim and soft halo around his shoulders and head. A group of ten people sat on the left side of the room and gazed at the man with silence and closed-mouth smiles.

Like the calm illumination of the sunrise, his long, golden brown hair reflected twinkles of light from the candles and was pulled out of his face with an ocean blue bandana. His beard was full and thick but groomed to perfection. His sharp features and thin face brought all focus to his crystal blue eyes, bright yet consumed with depths of darkness. He wore a short-sleeved, white shirt that hugged his body and showed every muscular intricacy. He tucked his shirt into flowing brown pants that almost resembled a skirt. He sat with a very calm and content expression, not at all affected by his surroundings.

Miles walked down the carpet and Samantha followed. Miles got to his knees and bowed. "Cyrus, I have brought to you a soul in need of freedom."

Next to Miles, Samantha came down to her knees. She looked up to the man's face, and his eyes stared into hers. He never broke eye contact. He sat in silence staring into her eyes longer than anyone had ever done, exposing her of every weakness. He lifted his hand slowly to her cheek and touched her face. He then said something that she would never forget. "You have so much beauty but not enough freedom to let in shine. What is your name?"

Samantha closed her eyes. She had never felt such a warm and loving touch in her life. She opened her eyes.

"I'm Samantha," she said.

"Samantha. This is your home now. Everything here is now yours since everything here is everyone's. We welcome you. In order to begin a new, free life, your new name will be Ivy. Is that okay with you?"

Cyrus put his hands out, palms up, and she slipped her hands onto his. He held them, softly rubbing his thumbs over her fingers, and looked into her eyes.

"I like Ivy," Samantha said.

At fourteen, she had finally found a place to call home. She was finally wanted. Her life had begun, right there in the depths of Freedom Park and in the heart of Freedom House, among the open redwood sky where the smell of baked bread and the sounds of animals were now her new sanctuary. She was no longer Samantha. She was Ivy.

CHAPTER NINETEEN

Her first month at Freedom House was euphoric and surreal. Everyone worked toward one unified goal. Cyrus called it the Journey to Freedom and anyone who arrived at Freedom House started in stage one: Entrance. However, there were three stages of the journey: Entrance, Compassion, and Free. Once these three stages of the journey were complete, they would all transcend into enlightenment, which Cyrus called true freedom and described as becoming one unit of harmony so strong they could change the world. All leaders and cultures would embrace compassion and love and all worldly problems would be resolved.

Samantha was ready to be part of something bigger; ready to experience compassion and love, two things she never had before arriving at Freedom House. Since Miles brought her there, he was to be her mentor. Miles was very close to Cyrus, always going on long walks with him to engage in deep conversation. Miles was responsible for keeping Cyrus' room in perfect condition. He wore a short-sleeved, white shirt and brown, loose pants. Miles was very tall, and his dark eyes kept a secret never told. He was to guide Ivy on their Journey to Freedom.

On the bench in the front of the koi pond, Miles and Ivy sat and Miles explained to her, "The Entrance phase is one of learning. We have wonderful activities and sessions here that will lead us all to the ultimate path, Freedom. We take pride in what we do here. You won't find anything like this on the outside."

"It all sounds so amazing," she said.

Miles gave her a smile. "Let's take a tour."

They started in the living room. The place for meditation sessions and where everyone slept. There were no televisions, computers, or phones allowed in Freedom House, so the living room was bare bones except for some pillows along the floor and a large, rectangular, blue and white rug. Because Cyrus believed that distractions would slow them down from their journey, there was nothing hung on the walls. Just bare, empty white space watching over them. Free of distractions, they only had themselves, their minds, and each other.

The living space had an open archway leading into the kitchen. Penelope, as Freedom House chef, was always prepping and cooking meals for each day. There were usually others on chore duty in the kitchen with her. Every day, fresh meals were cooked from a menu schedule each week. There was no alcohol, drugs, or tobacco allowed on the property. They were to feed their bodies and minds the purest foods and liquids. This would keep their minds clear of distraction. Samantha loved cigarettes but she would do anything to stay at Freedom House.

Opposite of the kitchen was another archway that led from the living room into the hallway. A long, thin, white rug ran down the depths of the hallway. At the end of the hallway, all the way down past the rooms, a red door faced them. The first door on the left was the yoga room. Miles opened the door and their faces lit up from the bright, large windows bare of curtains and a large, wooden floor that smelled of fresh lemon. There was a full body mirror that spanned the room. Each day, every person was required to do thirty minutes of yoga.

"Meet our yoga instructor, Skye. She has been with us from the beginning."

Skye had long, red, curly hair that was pulled back into a thick braid. Her bangs hung right over her eyebrows and she had dim freckles along her smooth, soft cheeks that looked like they were tossed gently onto her face. She wore a white bikini top with brown flowing pants. Her waist was bite sized, with small, muscular indentations that resulted from her yoga expertise.

"Welcome." Skye reached her hand to Ivy's face and caressed her cheek.

"We really believe in the power of breathing and movement. This brings peace to our minds and bodies and allows us to continue our journey," Skye said. "I'll see you later today for your first session."

"I've never done yoga. I'm not sure if I'll be any good," Ivy said.

"We will teach you. At Freedom House, we have no judgements. We are here all together for one purpose, to be set free from everything we have been taught about the world. You don't have to worry here. You'll never have to worry again," Skye said and hugged Ivy.

All that Ivy could say was, "Thanks." She'd be willing to give it a try.

Miles took Ivy next door to the bathroom and showed her where they showered. He watched Ivy as she scanned the open shower space filled with multiple showerheads. "We shower in groups altogether. We believe in the highest form of freedom absent from judgement. Doing everything together, builds our sense of community and we get to share the experience as one."

"Naked?" she asked.

Miles lips broke into an innocent smile, "Yes. But as Skye said, you will never need to worry while you're here. We're a family."

Across from the bathroom, there was only one door.

"We use this room for the Compassion stage of the Journey to Freedom."

Ivy's stomach held her breath hostage when Miles opened the door. Inside there was a skylight window, and light rays shone down angelically onto a large mattress overtaken by a fluffy white comforter and adorned with pillows of all sizes. Small throw rugs ran from the walls toward the mattress in the center. "Once you reach the Compassion stage, then we will come into this room together."

"It's...beautiful," she stared at it and couldn't help but think about the crammed and roach infested apartment she lived in before.

Miles closed the door and they both turned to face the end of the hallway. In front of them stood the red door.

"This door is always locked. Only Cyrus and a few others have access to it," Miles said.

"What's in there?"

"When your time is ready, you'll find out. Now it's time to learn about our daily schedule. Let's head back to the kitchen."

Freedom House ran on a structured schedule where everyone was either working for the community or participating in communal activities. Each person was assigned chores each day. Morning meditation began at 5:30 a.m. and was always led by Cyrus, who only came into the main house for meditation and sometimes went into the Compassion room. Anytime he entered the main house, he walked slow and observed everything around him. Sometimes he touched and smelled the flowers outside before entering or he would approach people and hold out his hands which was his way of welcoming with silent eye contact for minutes at a time. It was an honor to be approached by him. He had a way of making each person at Freedom House feel special. Members would crowd around him and follow him.

After morning meditation, it was shower time. Ivy was nervous at first, as her fourteen-year-old, premature body made her feel insecure. Everyone crowded to the bathroom. Each person helped one another get undressed, smiling and laughing together. Miles gently helped Ivy take her shirt off.

Ivy pulled her arms across her chest and crossed her legs tightly together as if she had to pee badly.

Miles put his hands on her shoulders. "Ivy, you don't have to be scared. I know this is new and different, but this is what freedom is all about."

He held his hands out and she unwrapped her arms and placed her hands on top of his. Hands locked together, Miles lifted their arms up into the air, bringing Ivy's arms with him. They stood under the water, their hands together and raised above their heads.

"Doesn't it feel great?" he asked.

She giggled and nodded her head as the water soaked her hair and dripped down her face and neck. The water hit her eyes and blurred her vision, but she could see Miles' smile. Ivy looked around and realized that everyone was having fun and was happy. No one was staring at her. No one was judging her. Each person had a partner who scrubbed the other clean and they laughed behind the lathered bubbles and shower heads that rained down on them.

After showers, everyone checked the schedule to see where they were assigned for the day and the schedule was the only thing hanging on the wall in the kitchen and in the entire house.

"Ivy, you're assigned to the garden. Head out to the front and I will meet you back here for lunch," Miles said and held his hands out, palms up, and she placed her hands into his. He held them with an intimacy of someone she knew for years.

She made her way out the front door, down the small stoned path, and to the garden. Standing in front of the garden was a young man wearing a white t-shirt and flowing brown pants.

"You must be Ivy. I have been expecting you. I'm Jonas."

Jonas reached out his hand and Ivy went to shake it. He pulled Ivy's hand up to his lips and kissed it.

"Welcome to Freedom House. This is our garden. We grow everything from tomatoes, to carrots, and lettuce, and broccoli. We must purify our bodies and minds."

CHAPTER TWENTY

After sobbing for an hour, Sophia kissed her father's forehead one last time.

"Bye daddy."

She turned around and started to walk down the aisle, past the empty pews, when she heard a sound. A distant, low music box perhaps. It was familiar and nostalgic. The twinkling chime of an ice cream truck melody was behind her. Sophia stopped and hesitated to look back. She closed her eyes and saw her sister Charlotte riding her purple bike down the street, her long, thick, black hair blowing across her face and flashing her great big smile.

She opened her eyes and saw the large church doors at the end of the aisle. The music stopped and she was relieved. Starting to walk down the aisle again, the melody started once more. Sophia turned around and standing outside the casket was her father. His skin was a pale purple color and it hung off his bones, flapping an inch down and swaying. Sophia's eyes widened before she shut her eyes and whispered to herself.

"Get it together. It's just in my head. Pull it together." But she could still hear the ice cream truck song.

"Soph," her father called out to her.

She opened her eyes and he was still standing in front of his casket in his clean black suit and tie, slicked back hair, and purple skin hanging off his bones. He moved down the aisle toward her except he didn't walk on his feet. When hitting the floor, each foot bent outward at the ankle, slipping and stretching out. He was walking on his ankles and bobbed up and down a little as he came down the aisle.

Sophia froze. She wanted to move back but she couldn't. When he got to her, he fell to his knees and pulled at her shirt.

"Why did you let Charlotte go? It was getting dark and you let her go," he cried into his hands.

Sophia slowly moved back. On his knees, crying into his hands, he looked up and pulled at his face. His fingers gripped the loose skin and he yanked it down like chicken skin slipping off meat. He pulled and screamed.

Sophia turned around and ran for the doors without looking back. Pulling the heavy door open, she threw herself out into the bright sunny day and slammed the door behind her. She ran down the church steps, got into her car, and cried the whole way home driving over Highway 17 back to Santa Cruz.

CHAPTER TWENTY-ONE

It was one of those days when the sunlight hits everything with just the right grace that it forces the world to know there exists something so much bigger out there. The light reflected off the koi pond, showering the surface with shimmering particles. The stone path leading to Cyrus' room settled in both sunlight and shadows, geometric shapes hovering over each stone. Miles and Ivy sat on the bench watching the black and orange koi swirl around each other under the water.

"Cyrus speaks about enlightenment, what he believes is true freedom. In meditation he leads us through visualizations. We know there are many on the outside that belong here with us. In these visualizations, we bring them home. Every person that comes to

Freedom House has manifested from these visions including you," Miles said, with a smile and a light in his eyes, but further into the depth of his gaze, trouble lived. Ivy knew that anguished stare all too well from her life on the outside.

"So, how are you adjusting to Freedom House?" Miles asked.

"I have never been part of something so important, so meaningful. I really feel like people care about me here. It's almost too good to be true but I know it is true and it's the best thing that has happened to me. My life before this was just shit. I hated myself and now I'm learning to love myself and love others. I can't thank you enough for bringing me here."

Miles stared down at the ground. His expression drastically changed from a gentle smile to one of concern. He wanted to say something, but an unknowable force stopped him. So, Ivy said something.

"What about you? How long have you been here?"

"Too long that I don't remember a life without this place. I have chosen not to remember. Things are pretty perfect here, but you know what they say, nothing is ever really perfect," he said, forcing a smile.

"What do you mean? Don't you love it here? I can't imagine going back to live on the streets or with my mother," said Ivy.

"Of course, I love it here. Who doesn't? We should really get back. Afternoon meditation will start soon. I'll meet you inside."

Miles quickly got up and began to walk back to Freedom House but after a few steps he stopped and looked back. "Ivy, you are beautiful no matter where you are. If you ever need anything you can always come to me. Just remember that, always come to me."

He disappeared into the house. She didn't understand then the fears that lived inside Miles. She wanted to find out, but she also knew she wanted to stay at Freedom House forever so a part of her didn't want to know. She stood up and began to follow Miles' path but stopped when she heard a screeching noise that was so piercing, she brought her hands over her ears to shield them. Ivy looked over and saw Penelope, in her white apron and underwear, slaughtering one of the pigs. Her fingers were in the pig's snout as she slit its throat. Streams of blood poured down the pig's pink skin, seeping into each crevice and wrinkle. Penelope's bare feet were sinking into the mud and blood soaked her toes, staining them red. She caught Ivy's stare, stood up straight, blood dripping down her hand as she held the knife to her side. She cocked her head to one side and smiled.

Ivy gave a smile and looked away. Walking back to the house, she could feel Penelope staring at her with that smile and with her bloody hands and feet. It wasn't until Ivy opened the backdoor of the house and went inside that she heard the pig squeal again.

CHAPTER TWENTY-TWO

Every day at 1:30 p.m., they all gathered in the living space for afternoon meditation and to hear Cyrus' teachings. They each lit a tealight candle and placed them around the room. Cyrus wore all white silk during meditation. Seated on the floor, legs crossed, they all waited for him to enter the house. Cyrus walked slowly into the living space, stopped at the entrance and intently stared at each of them, walked to the middle of the room and stood there.

"Thank you for allowing me to be part of your journey and making Freedom House a place of compassion and love. You are each very special in the Journey to Freedom and together we will change the world."

When he spoke, the hope in their eyes shone so bright and they felt the dreams in their hearts were possible through him. Because he believed in each of them, they just wanted to serve him.

"Meditation is essential in purifying our bodies and minds. Through meditation we can transcend anything, love and pain. Keep your focus on me and you will transcend. Take a deep breath, slowly at first. Take in every worry as you inhale. Now, slowly exhale through your mouth, letting your worries leave your body. Think of someone who has hurt you on the outside. Think of what they look like and what they did to you. Now, breathe in slowly. When you exhale, visualize sending that person a light so bright and a love so strong, like a mother gives to her baby."

Staring up at Cyrus from the floor, Ivy followed his every instruction but she didn't know about the light and love that a mother could give. She did know that Cyrus and everyone at Freedom House showed her these things. She imagined her mother and thought about the time she slapped Ivy across the face full force when Ivy asked for lunch money. Ivy pictured herself reaching out her arms high up to the sky and pushing light out of her fingertips to surround her mother. Ivy imagined all the love in the world piercing her mother's heart and imagined her happy and loving. In that moment, a heavy pain was lifted from Ivy and for the first time she didn't feel anger towards her mother, she felt sympathy.

Cyrus said, "Now we will move into our next meditation. Pain is just an illusion, something we are taught to avoid our entire lives. However, pain is unavoidable. We must embrace it and learn to transcend it, or we will not be able to help others and change the world. Let's begin."

Ivy turned to Miles. Miles gave her a sad look and smiled with his lips tucked in. He lifted his hands up and wrapped them around her delicate, tiny neck and slowly began squeezing, his grip gradually getting tighter. Her breath disappeared into herself and her body stiffened. Cyrus walked around looking down at each person, nodding his head in approval and wearing a smile.

CHAPTER TWENTY-THREE

Sophia was fourteen when her younger sister, Charlotte, age eight, went missing. They were playing in the cul-de-sac, which they referred to as the "U-ie." The "U-ie" was about five houses away from the Reys and was the usual hangout spot for the neighborhood kids. One summer day, Sophia and Charlotte had been riding their bikes for hours, checking in occasionally at home and using the opportunity to grab a snack or pick at the food their mom was cooking.

The sun was starting to set, and this was always their signal to start back home. As they began to ride down their street from the "U-ie," passing the McKinsey's, that's when they heard it, music to their ears, literally. It was the ice cream man.

Charlotte looked back at her sister while riding and said, "Sophia, I want one."

Sophia rode up next to her sister; they both put the brakes on and stood, holding the handlebars of their bikes. Charlotte had a purple mountain bike with a white basket in front but Sophia was older so she traded her kid bike in for a BMX, white with red trim.

"How much do you have?" Sophia asked.

Charlotte reached into the pocket of her jean shorts and pulled out some change, a red jolly rancher, and a small piece of paper crumpled up.

"Twenty-five cents."

Sophia searched her pockets and handed her sister fifty cents. "I'll wait here. Hurry up, mom will have a fit if it gets dark."

The ice cream man was now at the "U-ie" and parked right at the curb. One boy bought an ice cream but was already running back home. There were no other kids outside, as the entire neighborhood followed the "home by sunset" rule. Sophia watched as her sister rode back, about three houses away, and disappeared behind the truck, only pictures of ninja turtle pops, WWF vanilla bars, and popsicles could be seen.

As Sophia stared at the truck from a distance, she noticed something different about this one. The pictures of all the ice cream were peeling off in one corner and underneath was black paint. It was taking Charlotte longer than usual to get her Lemon Lime Ice Tickle. The truck began to move fully around the "U-ie" and picked up speed going down the street. Sophia's eyes followed the truck as it approached, about to pass her. Looking into the truck's window as it passed, she locked eyes for a second with the driver. She only made out dark, soulless eyes, and then the truck was gone.

She looked down the cul-de-sac. Lying on its side was Charlotte's purple bike and no Charlotte. Sophia rode over to it. She hopped off her bike and dropped it onto the curb. A foot away from Charlotte's bike was the change Charlotte was holding in her palm.

All Sophia could think was: *Why did I wait behind? Why didn't I just go with her?*

When Sophia went back home and led her parents to the "U-ie," her mother shrieked, falling to her knees and throwing herself over Charlotte's purple bike. The police taped off the neighborhood and the McKinsey's came out, standing on their lawn. Mrs. McKinsey held her hand over her mouth. The Jacksons also came out. So did the Hensens and the Smiths. Sophia sat on the curb in front of her house with bloodshot eyes and in a daze amongst the flashing police lights, the red and blue tinting the street, parked cars, and light poles. She told the police what had happened, but she wouldn't speak another word for a month.

CHAPTER TWENTY-FOUR

Pain meditation was an essential part of the Journey to Freedom. Cyrus believed that pain was essential in reaching enlightenment and without it, Freedom House would never get there. He told them that only special and intelligent people would be able to do it. Besides pain meditation, they also practiced pain yoga.

After her first pain meditation, Ivy was scared but she also felt free. She had come close to passing out, but she didn't. Right before she was about to go into darkness, Miles let go and she gained control again. She was nervous when she heard about pain yoga, but Miles assured her it was nothing she couldn't handle and was part of the Entrance stage. After a couple of months at Freedom House, pain yoga never got easier. Ivy reminded herself how much she wanted to serve the community and Cyrus, how much she wanted to be there, and how they all saved her from the outside.

She had just finished her morning chores and had an afternoon yoga session to get to. She walked to the doorway of the yoga room and stared in. About ten members were inside, standing straight with perfect posture on their blue mats, facing the large mirror in the front of the room. Each person wore the same expression on their face. Their eyes, absent from blinking, were in a calmed trance, eyebrows fully relaxed, with a closed-mouth smile. Skye stood at the front and gave the same hypnotized stare back at her students. She kept her body stiff and straight and turning her head, she looked at the doorway where Ivy stood.

"Ivy, we've been waiting for you. Close the door behind you."

Ivy stepped from the doorway into the yoga room and felt the extreme change in temperature inside the room. She immediately began to sweat, her palms getting clammy. She could barely take in a breath. Looking around, everyone stood on their yoga mats, and faced forward, like statues frozen in eternity.

The room was heated to 125 degrees Fahrenheit. Ivy couldn't think or breathe. There were rules during yoga. No one was allowed to leave the room during the thirty-minute session. No one was allowed to bring water into the room. If anyone needed to take a break, they could go into child pose position and that was it.

Skye had said, "These rules are in place to help us all and build our strength as a community, so that we are ready to be set free."

There was one large window absent of curtains that spanned the length of the wall opposite the door, peering out into the depths of the redwoods' deepest secrets. Skye held a small black device, home to a single button. When she pressed it, a thin black window screen slowly crept down from the top rim of the window to the bottom of the floor, immersing the room in total darkness.

"We will begin in tabletop position. Slowly curl your head back and keep your shoulders back. Let's move into cat pose, arch your back and shoulders, and keep your head down."

Ivy could barely breathe, and the combination of the heat and pitch-black darkness gave way to panic. Because she couldn't see anyone else, she couldn't tell if anyone else felt the same. She was starting to get dizzy but just kept moving her body, trying to keep up. Out of the darkness, a sliver of light and cool breeze broke into the room uninvited. Someone had broken the rule and left, opening the door hastily to escape. *Who was it?*

Skye interceded, "Please continue. Let's not let this cloud our bodies and minds. You are all so special and freedom is waiting for all of us."

After pain yoga, everyone was required to take a cold shower, turned all the way to the coldest setting. When the freezing water hit Ivy's back it sent shock waves through her skin and was almost unbearable, but she knew it would make her stronger. Ivy waited for everyone to be finished with showers and she waited for them to leave the bathroom so she could stay back alone. She looked at herself in the mirror. After getting through Pain Yoga, she felt accomplished, and a smile slowly came across her face. She thought about Cyrus and how he was like no one she had ever met. Her thoughts were interrupted by a whisper outside the bathroom, from down the hall. Ivy walked slowly to not be seen and hid near the bathroom doorway.

"Please, please let me try again. I don't want to go down there."

It was the voice of a middle-aged woman named Jody. She had been at Freedom House for some time and was in the pain yoga session with Ivy. In that moment, Ivy realized that Jody didn't shower with all of them. Ivy peered down the hallway, sticking out only the side of her face to look but not be seen.

"Jody, you know the rules. When you break the rules, there are consequences," said Cyrus.

Cyrus and Skye were standing with Jody at the very end of the hall, in front of the red door. Cyrus pulled out a key, unlocked the door, and they escorted her in, the door shutting very quietly behind them.

Later, they sat outside for dinner, near the koi pond, all fifty of the Freedom House members minus Jody. Penelope had made a meat stew with carrots, celery, and squash.

"This is tasty, what's this meat?" Ivy lifted her spoon up for Miles to see.

"That's Penelope's special ingredient."

"It's so good. I never got homemade meals at home. I mean on the outside."

"Penelope definitely has a gift. So, you on clean up duty after this?" Miles asked.

Ivy nodded and she stuffed her spoon piled with thick meat and carrots into her mouth.

After lunch, Ivy walked into the kitchen. Penelope was putting the leftovers away and Ivy got started on the dishes.

"Penelope, your stew was so good. I have never had anything like that. And your special ingredient was— "

Penelope slammed down a plate and looked at Ivy. "Who told you that?"

"I asked Miles what it was because— "

"Did he tell you?"

Ivy stopped washing but let the water run. "No, he just told me it was your special ingredient."

Her panic changed abruptly to a soft smile and she stared into Ivy's eyes. Picking up a dish, Ivy began washing again.

"What happened to Jody? I didn't see her at lunchtime," Ivy said.

"Who?" Penelope asked, with an excitement in her tone.

Ivy stopped washing again and thought maybe Penelope couldn't hear her over the sound of water running and the clanging of glasses.

Turning off the water, Ivy turned around and chuckled. "Jody. She was in yoga with us earlier today but not at lunch, where is she?"

Penelope tilted her head with that gentle smirk. "There's never been anyone by that name here. Are you feeling okay hun?"

Ivy's heart dropped to her knees. *Was she kidding?* Not knowing how to respond and wanting nothing more but to be out of that kitchen, Ivy said, "You're right. I have a bit of a headache. I'm going to head out to Freedom Park to get some air."

As she walked outside, she didn't turn around to look back at Penelope. She didn't have to. Penelope's stare and smile, that same one when she was slaughtering the pig, followed Ivy as she walked out. Ivy needed to find Miles.

CHAPTER TWENTY-FIVE

"The next update is on case number 59316, fourteen-year-old Samantha Watson. The mother last saw her the night of March 4. She said Samantha left for school that morning and never returned. She's been missing for three months. We've received some leads that have pointed us to what seems to be a commune out in Felton. We finally have a location. I'll be heading there to check it out tomorrow morning. Every month, about four girls in the Santa Cruz County region go missing. Some under-age and most from broken homes but not all. If this commune seems suspicious, we might be onto something. Any questions?" Detective Salvino scanned the room.

He stood at the front, a whiteboard behind him. There were chairs lined up classroom style and a group of officers sat and listened. An American flag hung in the far-right corner and photos hung along the walls of officers who had been killed in the line of duty.

"Yes, Officer Trenton?"

Trenton was a big guy and shaved his head down to the skin. "How sure are you that these girls might be living at this commune? Is the commune dangerous? I mean, let's face it, we might just be dealing with runaways who don't want to be found."

"Officer Trenton, when we have underaged girls missing, it doesn't matter if they chose to leave their families. It's our job to find them. It's also our job to locate the adults in charge of allowing these girls to stay with them as runaways. Yes, Officer Bailey?"

Bailey was young, thin, and had a buzzed military-style haircut. "Have these different leads led you to this one commune in Felton? If that's the case, then it seems likely that most of these girls could be there, but why? What is pulling them to that particular place?"

"That's exactly what we're here to find out. I will continue to lead this case, but I'll need to pull someone else in to support this one. To answer your question on what may be attracting them to this location, we don't know but if it's in fact true, it's concerning. Any other questions?"

"Yes, Officer Rey?"

"Detective Salvino, forgive me but don't you think we need to move a little faster on this? I was assigned to Faye Miller's case four years ago. She was fifteen when she went missing, and now, she's nineteen. The case went cold but if we're onto something here then we should move quickly on it."

"I agree. We are working strategically and as fast as we can. As you all know, we need to come up with a careful plan, one that won't jeopardize anyone's life. If there aren't any more questions, let's begin brainstorming."

Officer Trenton shouted out. "Let's raid the house. That always works."

He laughed, his mouth wide and open.

"We have to proceed with official protocol, or it will bite us in the ass later in a court situation. Any other winners?" Detective Salvino looked around without a smile.

"We can continue to chase those leads. They probably have more information than they're telling you," Officer Bailey said.

"We're definitely going to continue to investigate current leads and track down any others."

Officer Rey spoke up, "Why don't we send an undercover?"

The officers started to speak all at once.

"Alright, alright, enough. Quiet," Detective Salvino said.

"Boss, we all know what happened six years ago when we sent an undercover to work on the commune case up in Boulder Creek. We all know how it ended and I lost my partner." Officer Trenton wasn't laughing anymore.

Officer Rey said, "The case was blown wide open and at least it all came to an end. How many other kids would've suffered if we never sent anyone in there?"

They looked at Detective Salvino.

"Sending an undercover could be a good idea but, Officer Trenton is right, we don't want another Boulder Creek situation. We need to be preventive. We'd have to figure out who to send and act quickly on it."

Officer Sophia Rey stood up and said, "I can do it."

CHAPTER TWENTY-SIX

When Ivy found Miles, he was in Freedom Park scrubbing the stoned pathway leading to Cyrus' room. He was down on his knees, a red towel underneath them.

"Do you need some help?" Ivy asked.

"Only if you promise to sit with me during dinner later," he shot her a side glance and smiled, his black hair hanging in front of his face and his face shiny from sweat.

"I pinky promise."

He handed her a round, yellow sponge and she got down on her knees, dipped it into the bucket, and picked a stone to massage in circular motions. Foam bubbles collected around their hands as they scrubbed.

Ivy lowered her voice. "Miles, I have to ask you something."

Miles' hand stopped moving, he stared at the stone he was cleaning and didn't look up at her. Then he started scrubbing again.

"What's up?" he said.

"Where's Jody? She walked out of pain yoga yesterday and I saw her with Cyrus and Skye near the red door."

"She's just assigned to the Red Room for now," Miles said.

"But when I asked Penelope, she acted like Jody never existed here. Like she'd never knew anyone named Jody."

"Ivy, when people are assigned to the Red Room, it's serious, so Cyrus doesn't want it discussed. We are taught to forget about it in order to remove distractions. You understand?"

"So, Jody's okay?"

Miles locked eyes with her and said, "Of course she's okay. We shouldn't talk about this here."

For a few minutes in silence, they scrubbed the stones, the soft sound of their movement held their silence in the air.

Ivy broke it first. "Sooo, how do you think I'm fitting in here?"

"I've gotta say, I'm pretty impressed. You dived right in and Cyrus notices people who have that kind of dedication. You've already been here a few months, so you'll definitely finish The Entrance soon and move into the Compassion phase."

"I can't wait. I want to stay here forever. I've never had a family like this one before." Ivy reached her soapy hand onto Miles' and he looked up at her with gentle eyes and opened his mouth, about to say something but decided not to and continued scrubbing the stones.

"Let's finish these stones and get to feeding the animals," he said.

They fed the pigs the leftover stew that Penelope made. Ivy scraped the remaining vegetables and meat into the pigs' trough and said, "Miles, what were you going to say earlier?"

"When?"

"When we were cleaning the stones. You were going to say something but you stopped yourself," said Ivy.

"I'm not sure. I don't remember. I did need to talk to you though. Cyrus wants to see you today. Since I'm your mentor, I'll accompany you."

"Should I be worried?" Ivy stopped what she was doing and stared at Miles.

"Of course not," Miles said in a monotone voice, not even believing his own words.

"When?" Ivy asked.

"After we feed these pigs, let's wash up and head over to him. And don't worry. Things aren't always as they seem."

As she washed her hands, she thought about what Miles said. She had heard that many times, that things weren't always what they seemed, but up until this point, everything in her life seemed exactly what they were. Her life on the outside. Her mother. Those things were exactly as they seemed. Freedom House seemed to be the perfect place, a place where everyone was free and could be themselves with no judgements. Cyrus was like no one she had ever met or seen. Then, she looked up in the mirror while washing her hands and thought about Slim Steve. Like a sandcastle being pulled away into the sea, her heart swept away from her with the thought of him. He was the only one she missed. She wondered how he was doing.

"You ready Ivy?" Miles stood at the bathroom doorway.

"I've never been more ready," she said.

CHAPTER TWENTY-SEVEN

The needle flushed back with blood, smack entering inside veins and stealing more souls away into a liquid cloud of nothing. Slim Steve sat back on the same dirty and torn couch that he'd been nodding off on for the past three months. Day and night didn't exist in separate worlds anymore. They were intertwined into one long, eternal day that never ended. Time died away with his soul in that junky house.

He looked over at Cheddar.

"Have you seen Samantha?" Slim Steve asked.

Sitting on the couch, Cheddar's head was tilted back, his eyes were heavy and almost closed, his mouth open with drool trickling down his chin. Slim Steve nudged him.

"Cheddar! This is serious," he said.

"I told you, I'll re-up at 1:00."

"Naw man, have you seen Samantha? I haven't seen her in... a long time. She always comes around. I'm worried something happened to her. It's like she just disappeared."

"I don't know. You got a cigarette?"

"Didn't your brother disappear a while back?" Slim Steve asked.

"Benny? Yeah but he didn't really disappear. He came by and said he was moving. He left to live with some group. A common?" Cheddar said.

"You mean a commune?"

"Yeah, that too," Cheddar said, giving a silent, slow motion chuckle.

"So he told you when he left?"

"Yeah. He came by and said he was leaving. He told me he wouldn't be coming back and didn't want to talk to me again."

"That's fucked up," said Slim Steve.

"Do you have a cigarette?" Cheddar asked.

Slim Steve pulled out a cigarette, put it in his mouth, and then pushed another out and handed it to Cheddar.

"He said some shit about finally being free. I don't know. He's fuckin crazy," Cheddar said.

"Where is the commune?"

"How the hell should I know? He doesn't send me fuckin' post cards. Why? What's with all the questions Dr. Phil?"

"What if Samantha went somewhere like that? She wanted to runaway you know. Maybe we should go look for her," said Slim Steve.

"What's this *we* shit? Slim, she's just a kid. Kid's go through phases, get bored, then move on. She probably got bored of hanging with you on Pacific." Cheddar slow motion laughed again.

They sat there in silence for a while. The thick blanket hung over the living room window, creating a dark and musty room. There was no T.V. and the wallpaper was ripped, small pieces hung down from the tears.

Slim Steve whispered, "It wasn't like that. Sam and me, we were friends. I have to look for her."

He looked over at Cheddar only to find the redhead nodding off again. Leaning over him slowly, he reached into Cheddar's front pants pocket and felt a small rubber balloon. He held his breath and maneuvered with ease, taking it out. He knew Cheddar was still holding. He would shoot up first, then go look for Samantha.

CHAPTER TWENTY-EIGHT

Walking down the stone path to Cyrus' room, Ivy took a deep breath. They walked through the doorway and into the dimly lit room, tealight candles surrounding the perimeter. There were six members sitting on the floor on each side of the room, staring at Cyrus with concentration.

At the end of the narrow carpet, he sat crossed-legged, his long golden hair hanging down his shoulders. He stared at Ivy as she walked down the carpet with Miles. A still expression was across his face like a mannequin and he kept both palms pressed together right under his chin.

"Sit with me Ivy."

Ivy could feel her pulse racing so fast that her temples throbbed against the sides of her head and she tried to catch her breath, but it disappeared momentarily. Cyrus gestured for her to sit in front of him. Bringing herself to the floor, she sat crossed-legged and faced him. All eyes were on them as the other Freedom House members watched from the sidelines. Ivy thought again, for a moment, about what Miles said. *Things aren't always what they seem.* Right now, she wasn't sure at all what this seemed like or what it was, but she wanted to understand.

"Ivy. I have been noticing you. You are one of the youngest here at Freedom House, yet your wisdom and beauty far exceed your youth. Everyone here at Freedom House has a purpose. Some are here to help with the daily chores and others are meant to work directly with me, like Miles, Skye, and Penelope. I would like you to work more closely with me. I'd like you to be my secretary. You will make sure Freedom House is on track, schedules are on time, and that everyone is moving quickly in our Journey to Freedom. We will need everyone to be at the same stage very soon. We must prepare for this and I need your help. Are you ready to move to the Compassion stage?"

Facing Cyrus, Ivy only moved her eyes, first to the left then down to her legs. Her heart beat through her entire body, pumping through her nerves. She knew she'd have to answer.

"I am more than ready Cyrus." Her words slipped out of her mouth with confidence.

"That is great to hear. Miles, bring Ivy her new clothing."

Neatly folded clothes were in Miles' hands. There was a bikini top similar to Skye's and brown loose pants.

Cyrus smiled. "Ivy, put these on."

"Thank you, I'll put them on right away."

"Put them on here, right now," he said and touched her knee.

This time, Ivy turned to look around at the members sitting, watching. Their expressions hadn't changed at all. Ivy looked down at the clothes she was wearing.

Miles held his hand out to her. "I'll help you."

In the middle of Cyrus' room, standing on the long carpet, Miles lifted Ivy's shirt above her head. She pulled her pants down and tried to hide her tiny, adolescent breasts. Cyrus stood up, walked over to Ivy, close enough for her to feel his breath, and he said, "Ivy, you never have to be ashamed here. You are beauty. Everyone here is beauty."

With that mannequin smile, he held his hands out and she placed her hands into his. Lifting her hands high above their heads, they placed their palms together and stood there with Ivy naked for all to see.

"Welcome to the Compassion stage."

Cyrus received the clothing from Miles and put the bikini top on her, tying the back. It was the first time in her life she felt beautiful. She put on the brown pants and Cyrus said, "Since Miles has been your mentor, he will be the one to introduce you to the Compassion room."

Miles was right. Things weren't what they seemed. Her dreams were coming true at Freedom House. She found a family and was finally important and needed by people. That night, she could barely sleep. She was lying on the floor in the living space, Miles was asleep to her left and Penelope to her right. Their arms and legs touched, with little space to move. All the members of Freedom House slept here. Only occasional snores could be heard in the dark room.

Ivy lay there thinking about how Cyrus chose her. She wondered what the Compassion room would be like. Amongst her thoughts and the stillness of the room, she heard something. The sound was rhythmic, but she couldn't make out what it was. *Was it an animal outside?* Lying there and listening, she tried to make sense of what it was. She pushed herself up using her hands and avoided waking anyone. Moving her feet and legs as slow as she could, she stood up and stepped around the sleeping bodies on the floor.

She walked toward the kitchen. The sound got further away. She turned around and faced the hallway and the darkness disappeared around the corner. Turning down the hallway, the red door stood at the end and challenged her. The sound was louder. *Was it music?* She moved one foot in front of the next, placing her toes down first and then gradually placing her heel down.

The yoga room door was closed. As she walked past the bathroom, which didn't have a door, she caught a glimpse of herself in the mirror, a dark blurred figure creeping through the night. Approaching the red door, she heard that sound again. Down into the unknown depths through the red door, girls were softly chanting but she couldn't make out exactly what they were saying. *Why would they be singing in the middle of the night?* Ivy reached for the doorknob just on the chance that it might be unlocked. Her fingers gripped the knob and she inhaled deeply and started to turn it when someone behind her whispered,

"Ivy, what are you doing?" It was Miles.

A jolt of energy jumped up into her body pushing her shoulders into a spasm. The scream that grew inside her within that second and about to escape was forced back down.

"What the fuck, Miles. You scared me. Don't you hear that sound?"

"Ivy, you know you are supposed to be in the living space sleeping."

Ivy turned to face Miles, the red door behind them, watching them, "Miles, what really happened to Jody? What's in there?"

"Look, Ivy, I don't want you to get…in trouble or anything. We need to go back to the living space."

"What's inside this room?"

"There's a lot that goes on here that people don't know about. Things that you will find out along the way. Ivy, I really care about you."

Then Miles leaned in close to her ear, the heat of his breath shot down her neck. "I made a mistake bringing you here. You should get out before it's too late."

She couldn't believe what she was hearing. What was Miles trying to hide from her and why would he want her to leave.

"How could you say that? This is my home now. You brought me here."

"Ivy, please don't take it wrong. I'm just trying to protect you."

"You're just jealous that Cyrus is giving me more attention."

"It's not like that," Miles said, shaking his head and staring at her with a sadness that suffocated his eyes.

"Just leave me alone. I don't want to talk about this anymore," Ivy said.

"I'm sorry if I upset you. Please come back to bed soon."

Miles turned around and walked back to the living space as Ivy stood there, shocked that her mentor was trying to get her to leave Freedom House.

That's when Ivy saw it, someone's single eyeball peeking through the crack of the door from the Compassion room. The door slowly shut, and the eye disappeared behind it. Someone had been watching them.

CHAPTER TWENTY-NINE

Tonight was the night. It was Ivy's introduction to the Compassion room, but her excitement turned to dread after what had happened the night before. She didn't understand how Miles could bring her to Freedom House only to tell her to get out.

During breakfast, Ivy sat with some new people, the same group that could always be found in Cyrus' room, always in an entranced meditation. They ate on the stone path that led to his room, just far enough from the others to be secluded but close enough to observe them all.

"Ivy, congratulations on becoming Freedom House's secretary. That is such an important role here. Are you excited about tonight?" said Jonas.

As Jonas was speaking, Ivy stared into his eyes hoping to catch any look of suspicion, her attempt to find out if Jonas was the one watching her and Miles the night before.

"Ivy?"

Ivy snapped out of thought. "Thanks, I'm very excited. I've been waiting for something like this."

Suspicion didn't accompany them while they sat under the bright, blue sky. Ivy breathed out relief.

"So, what's your first task as secretary?" Jonas said.

"I'm not sure. After breakfast I have a meeting with Cyrus."

"Well, congratulations again. We have to honor the rare opportunities in life, otherwise they float past us and move on to someone who's ready to catch them," Jonas said.

"I've never met anyone like him before. Where is he from anyway?" Ivy asked.

"The past is only a fragment of time that is now gone Ivy. What matters is that he's here now. He was brought here to teach us about the Journey to Freedom. He is the only one who can lead us there," Jonas said with big, bright eyes of certainty.

"I never knew I could be free until I came here," Ivy said.

"You're really going to enjoy the room of Compassion. It'll get you closer to freedom and closer to everyone here. You're going to learn that at Freedom House, it doesn't matter if you're alive or dead because there's something so much bigger that exists inside each of us, inside you Ivy," Jonas said as he reached his hand to her cheek.

Ivy placed her hand over his and held it at her cheek.

"Thanks Jonas. I have to meet with Cyrus. Thanks for the talk." Ivy stood up and started walking down the path to Cyrus' room.

"Ivy," Jonas said.

Looking over her shoulder, Ivy stopped walking and Jonas sat cross- legged on the ground.

“Every place you encounter, there will be people who want to stop you, to bring you down. Just remember, rare opportunities are sometimes only presented once. It’s what you do with it that determines your fate. Cyrus is God’s gift to us and we must show our gratitude,” Jonas said.

“I understand,” Ivy said, and she walked to Cyrus’ room.

Entering the doorway of Cyrus’ room, Ivy stopped and looked down at the long, white carpet that rolled down the room and to Cyrus sitting on the floor.

"Beautiful Ivy, come forward," Cyrus said, articulating every letter, every syllable.

There were members sitting to the left and right of the rug, just staring at Cyrus with the faintest of smiles. Their silence and stillness made them seem nonexistent. The room was dark as always with candles lit along the walls.

Ivy walked down the carpet and sat down in front of Cyrus, crossing her legs, mirroring his seated position.

"Ivy, we need to begin faster preparations to move everyone into the Free stage. I know tonight is your first night in the room of Compassion, but you need to understand that we must move quickly. Last night, I had a vision. The darkness is coming. If we do not complete our Journey to Freedom soon, we will all be consumed by this darkness. I will be making an announcement in today’s evening meditation session."

"I understand. What do you need me to do?" Ivy asked.

"You will need to revise the daily schedule. Add an additional pain meditation and an additional pain yoga to each day. We need a total of four pain practices each day. Ivy, your help with this is more important than you know. Freedom House is going to change the world."

"That’s why I came here Cyrus.”

A smirk formed across his face, breaking through his pensive stare at Ivy.

"There is one more thing. Everyone needs to be placed into the room of Compassion. You'll need to create a schedule for The Compassion room and make sure all members are introduced to it within the next two days. Most have been already, but there are still some new members who haven't."

"I can do that."

"I know you can. You are very special Ivy," Cyrus said, looking into her eyes. His stare moved past her skin and into the depths of her body. He leaned in and placed his hands on her waist.

"We cannot let the darkness consume us Ivy," he said, and his touch sent chills up her back.

As she walked back down the white carpet to exit, Ivy couldn't stop thinking about how important this was to her and to Freedom House. She thought about the darkness that Cyrus spoke of and wondered when it would come. She thought about the darkness she lived in for so long on the outside and how Jonas was right, this was her chance to be part of something bigger.

Ivy walked into the kitchen and Penelope was chopping squash.

"Hey Penelope."

"Hello Ivy. Are you feeling better today?" She continued to chop.

"So much better. Thanks for asking," Ivy said.

"That makes me happy to hear."

Ivy watched Penelope chopping the squash. She chopped with her right hand and held the squash securely with her left. Her left fingernails caught Ivy's attention. They were soaked in red with dark grime under her nails. She was leaving pink fingerprints on the squash. The chopping sound stopped.

"Something wrong Ivy?" Behind her smirk was a joke only she was aware of.

"Um, no, not at all."

"Perfect."

She continued chopping. As Ivy began to walk away, Penelope started to hum a song. It made Ivy stop but she forced herself not to turn and look back at Penelope. *Why was that song so familiar?* The realization knocked the wind out of Ivy. It was the same chanting sound she heard the night before behind the red door. She took a breath and continued to walk away. Ivy knew she had a lot of work to get started on and couldn't let anyone or anything get in her way.

It was finally time. Ivy had to meet up with Miles and begin her introduction to the room of Compassion. She wasn't looking forward to seeing him. They met in Freedom Park at the koi pond. On the bench, he sat, staring into the pond. Ivy sat next to him, not saying anything.

"This has always been my favorite place at Freedom House. The koi have been here since the beginning as well," he said.

"Miles, about last night, I still don't understand," said Ivy.

"One died today," Miles said, and continued to look at the pond.

"What?"

"I found a fish, dead. I took it out with a net. At least it's finally free."

"Miles, I'm sorry I said you were jealous. I just don't get where this is coming from. You brought me here."

"I know what I did. Are you ready for the room of Compassion?"

"I am more than ready but I want to know—"

"You'll understand soon Ivy," Miles stood up and held out his hand. They walked together to the Compassion room.

Beauty comes in many forms and sometimes it wears a mask that fools people. Sometimes it wears a mask that pretends to comfort. Miles opened the door to the room of Compassion. The ceiling was heightened to the heavens, so high up with a skylight at the very top where brightly lit stars shimmered, and the universe watched over them. Transparent cloth hung down the mattress frame in a repeating pattern, inviting and protective. Ivy ran her fingers along it, the cloth was smooth and light as air. Long skinny carpets were laid out all around the room and led to the bed. There was nothing on the walls. In the far, left corner, was a beautifully carved wooden wardrobe with two doors. To the far right, was a doorway that led into a room with marble floor and one large white porcelain bathtub. An overwhelming scent of flowers filled the air.

Miles closed the door behind him and locked it. They were the only ones in the room.

"Let's sit Ivy."

Sitting on the mattress, Ivy placed her hands in her lap, knees tightly pressed together.

"Ivy, I'm sorry about last night but I'm only trying to protect you. There's a lot that goes on here that you don't know about."

"Like what? Everything here is perfect. I had no life worth living before Freedom House," said Ivy.

"This room, the room of Compassion, is to prepare you for Cyrus. To be with Cyrus. Don't you understand?"

"And what's so wrong with that? Cyrus is like no one I've ever met. He knows things."

"Ivy, when a person enters this room, they are being groomed for Cyrus. He is very particular in what he wants. He has all the mentors prepare new members. You're only fourteen. I didn't know he was putting young girls in here until he asked me to bring you in here."

"Cyrus knows I'm beautiful, so I feel special. Like he says in meditation, we are one and together we must become free. This is just all part of the bigger picture. If he wants a special night with me, I have to show gratitude for that."

"Ivy, I won't do it. You're fourteen. This isn't okay. Think about it if you were on the outside. It's completely wrong."

"But we're not on the outside anymore Miles. We are doing something bigger here. It's not like I'm being forced, I want it."

"I'm not going to prep you. You are a wonderful girl, but you don't deserve what's coming."

"Cyrus deserves it and so do I. I've waited my entire life to be important. You can't take this away from me. I guess I'll need to tell Cyrus to assign me a new mentor."

"You know if you do that, I will face the consequences," Miles voice cracked from concern.

"Then prep me."

"Ivy, I really like you, but this isn't right."

"It's my job to help Freedom House move closer to enlightenment. Cyrus said it himself. If you don't prep me, I will have someone else do it."

Miles' eyes filled with tears. His lips were tightly sealed as he held back the pain but a tear broke free; a small droplet fell over his bottom waterline, starting out slow and picking up speed as it dripped down his cheek. He slowly lifted his hand to his face and wiped it.

"I can't let someone else do that to you. Just know Ivy, I am forever sorry."

Miles walked over to the wooden wardrobe. Grabbing both knobs, he opened it widely. On the top two shelves there were bottles of different sizes and colors filled with liquids. Ivy's eyes ran across in awe and she caught a word across one of the bottles. *Lube.* She wasn't sure what it was.

On the bottom shelves there were objects she had never seen before, but they looked interesting. Some were bright pink, some just plain black. Some had round circular shapes attached, and others were long and cylindrical.

Ivy walked over and grabbed one. "I like this one."

In silence, Miles grabbed one of the lube bottles. They went back to the mattress and he helped her get undressed, then he did too. He looked into Ivy's eyes, reached his hands gently to her face, and said, "I am so sorry Ivy."

CHAPTER THIRTY

She was awakened by the rays of the sun bursting through the skylight. Miles was still asleep to her right, his muscular chest rising and falling slowly from each breath. He looked content.

Ivy looked up, out the skylight, staring at the blue morning sky and the white cotton clouds. Jonas was right. The room of Compassion had changed her life. She felt connected to something bigger.

She lifted herself up using her arms; her body was sore. She moved the white canopy curtains away from her face and carefully stood up and walked to the bathroom with small steps and stiff knees. Sitting on the toilet, Ivy waited for the release and when it came, it stung. She wiped and there was some blood but nothing unbearable.

She still didn't understand what Miles was so worried about. Last night was just another form of love, compassion, and pain practice. Everything they needed to prepare them for their Journey to Freedom. This was why Freedom House was so special and so beyond everything on the outside. Cyrus understood the way to enlightenment, and they were going to change the world and change the mindset of everyone out there. Ivy couldn't wait to join Cyrus in the Compassion room. She couldn't wait to help others experience the same thing she had last night.

Ivy's thoughts were interrupted when she heard a loud pounding, but it wasn't coming from the Compassion room's door. It was faint, and a little farther away. A muffled voice. Ivy walked to the bedroom door, slow and steady as to not make a sound. Her hand reached for the doorknob and she focused on turning it and then moved the door open just a crack. Someone was knocking aggressively on the front door. Ivy stayed inside the room of Compassion and listened from there.

"This is the police. Anyone home?"

The police? Why were they here? What did they want? Ivy had a lot of experience with police officers on the outside. Each month, the neighbors would call the cops on her mom and whatever boyfriend she chose to bring home to teach her a lesson.

One Friday night, Samantha was watching T.V. in the living room. There was no ceiling light, just an old, dirty lamp that flickered in the corner of the room. They had one couch with a faded orange and white floral print, and it reeked of cigarettes. Samantha sat on the floor watching her show.

There was a small doorway that led into the kitchen; the kitchen that was never used for cooking. In the sink, dishes were stacked high. A four-story luxury food condo for bugs. Samantha never witnessed her mother clean the counters. There was grime built up in the crevices of each tile. Sometimes you could catch a glimpse of a cockroach running by. That Friday night, it started out with a small argument.

"I can go now," Samantha's mother, Darleen, slurred.

"You're always waiting till the last fuckin' minute. You're lazy," said boyfriend number three, the mechanic alcoholic named Steve.

"I'm sorry baby, I'll go right now and buy some food."

She walked out of the kitchen doorway and Samantha looked over at her. Darleen's eyes caught Samantha's as she held a short glass of vodka. She forced an innocent smile, looking like a child that just got into trouble.

"No you fuckin won't," Steve said and grabbed her hair as she walked out of the kitchen and pulled her with all the strength he had. Her body flew back onto the kitchen floor like a rag doll. The small drinking glass she was holding shattered on the kitchen floor.

"Steve, please, please not again."

"I told you too many times already Darleen. Now it's time to teach you a Goddamn lesson," he yelled.

The neighbors pounded on the wall. Samantha stood up slowly, her knees weak and her heart pounding out of her chest.

"Sit down brat," he yelled at her.

Samantha's normal Friday night thoughts began to pay a visit. Was he going to kill her? Was she going to get hurt? Would the police finally save them?

"Leave her alone," Darleen said, her voice absent of inflection and paralyzed by booze.

"Shut up," Steve said, standing over her as she lay there, her dirty, white tank top strap hanging down her arm. He punched her into the floor. There was a loud pounding on the front door. They all knew who it was.

"Police, open up now!"

Steve got one last punch in before stopping. He grabbed a dish towel from the kitchen, wiped his knuckles, and tossed it onto Samantha's lap. "Get rid of it."

Darleen grabbed onto the edge of the kitchen counter to lift herself up while Samantha went over to her. "It's not a big deal Samantha."

They could hear Steve talking to the police officer through the living room, but they couldn't see them.

"We received a call about a disturbance."

"Nothing exciting happening here officer," Steve said.

"Have you been drinking sir?"

"Is it a crime to drink in the privacy of your own home?"

"Can we take a look around?"

Darleen looked at Samantha and raised her pointer finger to her lips, signaling her daughter to not make a peep.

"If you don't have a warrant then you're not welcome here," said Steve.

"Then keep it down. I don't want to be called out here again."

"Ivy?" Miles was awake.

Ivy's mind came back to reality and she placed her index finger to her lips, signaling him to stay quiet.

They heard the voice again. "Police. Open up!"

Someone must have made their way to the front door because they heard the door open.

"Good morning sir, how can I help you?" Penelope said.

"Good morning to you as well miss. I'm Detective Salvino. You may be able to help me. A young girl, fourteen years of age, went missing about five months ago. Her name is Samantha Watson. She was last seen downtown on Broadway and 7th Street, about fifteen miles from here. Here's a picture of her, have you seen her?"

"What a lovely name. Salvino. Is that Italian?"

"It is and thank you. Can you take a look at this picture?"

"Well that's just devastating. I can't imagine how her parents are feeling? I've never seen her before. I wish I could be of more help, detective," Penelope said slowly with a hint of flirtation.

"Thank you, miss. If you happen to hear anything at all, please give me a call. Here's my card."

"Of course. I really hope you find her. There are so many bad people out there."

"Thank you and what was your name again?" Detective Salvino said.

"Claire."

"You have a nice day, Claire. Please reach out if you hear anything."

"Have a wonderful day as well, Detective Salvino." Ivy and Miles could hear Penelope closing the front door.

Ivy closed the bedroom door and looked at Miles. He put his hands onto her shoulders.

"Ivy, this is your way out, your ticket home," he said.

"Freedom House is my home. I'm not leaving Miles so you can stop trying to convince me."

"What if that detective comes back?" Miles said.

"We need to tell Cyrus. He'll know what to do," Ivy said.

Miles turned away from Ivy, grabbed his clothes and put them on without saying a word. He opened the door, walked out of the room, and closed the door behind him. She didn't care that he was upset. She was more worried about Detective Salvino. Ivy walked over to the bed to get her clothes on and heard a knock on the door.

"Miles leave me alone please."

"It's Penelope."

"Oh, then come in."

Penelope opened the door and carefully shut it behind her. She held out a business card. "Someone's looking for you."

Ivy grabbed it:

Santa Cruz Police Department
Detective Emilio Salvino
155 Center St.
Santa Cruz, CA 95060
831-752-2448

"I heard. We have to go to Cyrus right away," Ivy said.

"I was thinking the same thing," Penelope said.

CHAPTER THIRTY-ONE

Ivy and Penelope sat on the floor in front of Cyrus.

"I answered the door and told the detective I had never heard of a Samantha Watson. He gave me this card," Penelope said, and handed it to Cyrus.

He calmly took it and read it, the slightest smile across his lips.

"When he asked your name, what did you say?" His eyes didn't leave the card in his hand.

"I told him my name was Claire."

"Penelope, you did the right thing, that's so smart. Did he seem convinced?"

"Oh yes, he has no idea about anything."

"Perfect. We wouldn't want anything to get in the way of our Journey to Freedom. The people on the outside do not understand. They only care about the insignificant conventions they have been taught. Ivy, you may be fourteen, but you are a wise soul, a soul that needs to be part of this journey."

"Thank you, Cyrus," Ivy smiled.

"I will keep this. You did the right thing Penelope but when Detective Salvino comes back, we need to have already completed our Journey to Freedom. We need to move faster than anticipated. Ivy, get me Miles. We will work out a strategy with him."

"Right away Cyrus," said Ivy.

"Great. We cannot waste any time. Ivy, do not let this stop your work. We have to continue to move everyone along. I want Freedom House ready in two weeks or less if possible."

Penelope leaned over and kissed Cyrus on his lips. Ivy did the same. When she moved her lips off his, he grabbed her and kept her close to his face. "Ivy, I know you will not disappoint me," he said.

"Detective Salvino, she's never gone undercover," Captain Malone said. "I think it's premature. We can't have another Boulder Creek situation."

"Captain, I understand your concern. These communes feed off men and women, but their sweet spot are women. Boulder Creek was unfortunate but we both know they were more than a commune. Their leader got his power by sucking the life out of weak souls. By the time we got there, it was too late. We can't be too late with this one. Officer Rey is the only female officer I believe who can pull this off. We only need a week or two, but we need to get her there now. I know they're hiding something."

"Salvino, you do whatever it takes to find those missing girls, but you better find them alive. It's you who will have to live with it."

"Thank you, Captain."

Detective Salvino called another strategy meeting. A large cork board was to his left as he stood at the front of the room, and hanging on the board were nine pictures, all young girls smiling for their school pictures.

"Let's talk Boulder Creek. We need to run through what happened there and make sure we don't make the same mistakes."

Detective Salvino pointed to the whiteboard where he had written some bullet points in black pen. "It started out the same. We were dealing with under-aged girls who were disappearing every month. When we found the Boulder Creek commune, we spoke to two women. They denied there were any under-aged girls and boys there. What did they believe in? They all preached a life of unification, a shared kind of living. They were not suspicious in any way. All our leads kept pointing us to that cabin out in Boulder Creek, but we had nothing on them, until it was too late. I got the call on August 5th. There had been a brutal home invasion resulting in bloodshed near the college campus. Five beaten and stabbed to death. The victim that the intruders went easy on was stabbed thirty-six times. By the time we got back to Boulder Creek, the entire commune had hung themselves in that house. When we arrived, all you could see were bodies hanging from the ceiling. We found nine under-aged missing girls and six boys. The point is, we acted too slow. When they're ready to strike, these cults move fast. We must be faster."

Officer Bailey said, "So how do we get Officer Rey inside the Felton commune?"

"That is exactly why we're here. We need some ideas and we need them fast."

Officer Rey thought about Charlotte. She thought about the purple bike on the curb of the "U-ie," the front wheel spinning solo, the sun setting behind it.

"Officer Rey? You okay?"

"Yes sir," Sophia said.

"Any thoughts on how we get you in there?"

"You said Samantha Watson was last seen at the market on Broadway and 7th. That means some of these commune members are coming into town for water and food. Let's assign someone to go out there to track the house and follow whoever leaves. Eventually someone will have to do another food run. If this is the commune we're looking for, they prey on people who've lost their way, right? Put me outside the store and I can beg for money. Then maybe I'll get an invite back to the commune."

"I can track the house," Officer Bailey said.

"That could work. Officer Rey, while Bailey is out there you and I can go over undercover protocol, but we won't have a lot of time. We must work quickly."

"Not a problem," said Officer Rey.

"Officer Bailey, start procedure. Use one of our civilian cars. Directions to the house are in my office, on my desk."

Officer Bailey stood up and looked at Officer Rey. "You got this. Let's bring this one down."

He walked out, head high, and his fists clenched.

"Bailey," said Detective Salvino.

Officer Bailey turned around with a stern look.

"Don't get caught out there."

Officer Bailey didn't say a word. He nodded his head down once, turned around, and walked out.

"Sophia, are you sure you're ready for this?"

"I've been ready for years, detective."

"You need to understand these places always have a leader. You will need to identify that person quickly before they harm anybody."

"How will I communicate with you while I'm there?"

"You'll take a small cell phone and you will need to hide it. Officer Rey, in some undercover cases, the cop at least is armed with a waistband firearm, unless one is going in deeper. In this case, you will not be armed."

Sophia moved only her eyes up to look at Detective Salvino.

"I can manage that," she said.

"We'll need to wait for Bailey's call with the store location. Once you're set up outside the store, how do you plan to engage the person?"

"I have an idea. Get me a female officer," Officer Rey said.

Sophia's plan was crazy but not as crazy as going undercover into Freedom House. No weapons and little communication. The undercover procedures to be followed made it even more of a challenge to not get caught. If substances were offered, they were to be refused. Under no circumstances is an undercover to engage in sexual activity of any kind or to expose any private part. Clear communications were a must and had to be planned out ahead of time. But now, it was Sophia Rey's time to save these young girls, something she couldn't do for her little sister.

A female officer appeared in the doorway, her blonde hair pulled back into a tight bun.

"Detective Salvino, Officer Rey. The Captain said you needed me." Officer Deanna Morris said upon entering, hands to her waist.

"Hello Officer Morris, thank you. We have a serious undercover case that Officer Rey will be working on. She won't be armed. That's as much as I can disclose. We have a plan on how to get her into the location," Detective Salvino said.

"What can I do to help?" asked Officer Morris.

"I need you to punch me as hard as you can. I need you to give me a black eye," said Officer Rey.

Officer Morris chuckled, looked at Detective Salvino, then at Officer Rey. Her chuckle was interrupted by her own realization—they were dead serious.

CHAPTER THIRTY-TWO

Ivy lit the candles in the living room. Pain practices had now been increased to five times daily. Cyrus was allowing new members in but only if it was an extreme situation, and in two days there was to be no more recruiting. All the candles were lit, and their small flames flickered with shadows tapping the walls. Penelope came into the living room wearing her usual white apron and panties. Her apron had pink fingerprinted stains from wiping her hands on it as she cooked.

"Cyrus asked me to set plates out on the floor," Penelope said. Small portions of meat were on each plate.

"Wonderful. I can help," Ivy said.

"I'm glad you've come to enjoy it here Ivy. You've become a big part of Freedom House."

"It's the home I've never had."

"Me too," said Penelope.

Cyrus sat in the middle of the living space, everyone else sat around him.

"There is a Darkness coming for us. It's coming to stop us, to stop our Journey to Freedom. We must stop it first. Today marks everyone's entrance into the Free stage. In eight days, we will complete our Journey to Freedom. We must strengthen our minds and bodies. Pick up the plate in front of you."

Miles lifted his plate and Ivy could feel his stare in her direction.

"Penelope made this for all of us. Today, we eat this together to enter the Free."

Ivy looked down at the cooked meat, the smell entered her nostrils and shot down into her stomach, making her stomach turn.

"Take a bite, all as one," Cyrus said.

Using her fingers, Ivy picked it up as everyone else did, and they all took a bite. The meat was tough in texture. The repetitive chewing motions exhausted Ivy's jaw and the meat stayed one moist blob in her mouth, never getting smaller.

"I know you have all been wondering what happened to Jody. Jody has made a great sacrifice for Freedom House. She has helped us get to the stage called The Free. Today we are eating the meat of Jody. She sacrificed herself so that each of us could nourish our bodies with one of our own."

Ivy stopped chewing and she looked around, but everyone else continued to move their jaws, chomping at the meat in their mouths called Jody. Ivy almost vomited but forced herself to keep it down. She heard a gurgling sound and looked over in that direction. Jonas was vomiting into his own lap. Cyrus walked over to him and placed a hand on Jonas' shoulder.

"That's quite all right, Jonas. This is normal. We cannot waste though. Penelope, get a spoon," Cyrus said.

Ivy started to chew again while looking over at Cyrus and Jonas. Ivy could only think one thing. *There was no way he was going to ask him to scoop it up and eat it, was there?* Ivy believed in Cyrus, but how did this fit into their Journey?

Penelope skipped through the kitchen and back into the living room with a big smile and handed Cyrus a spoon. He held the spoon pointed straight up, in front of Jonas' face. Jonas, pale with saliva down the corner of his mouth, took the spoon.

Cyrus smiled, "Smile Jonas, this is what we all need. Don't waste. Scoop it up and eat it."

Jonas looked down at the chunky liquid on his lap. He took a scoop and brought it to his mouth. At that moment, Ivy looked away but the sour smell of Jonas' vomit, of Jody's cooked insides, lingered in the air.

"I'll help you eat it Jonas. We're in this together," Penelope said.

Penelope got onto her knees in front of Jonas and opened her mouth, a signal to Jonas to feed it to her. Jonas lifted the spoon, the liquid swayed to the edges almost spilling over from Jonas' shaking hand. He placed the spoon on Penelope's lips and tilted it into her mouth. Penelope slurped it down and before finishing it, a small chunk of Jody meat vomit was on the corner of her mouth. She used her pink-stained index finger to push it into her mouth and sucked her finger a little too long.

"Here's the flip phone. It'll be your one and only source of communication with us. You'll need to hide it. What we usually suggest is for you to tape it to your body, then when you are in the location, find a spot to keep it hidden. Maybe underneath a floorboard. Or behind the toilet. It's up to you, just don't let it get discovered. You aren't required to call, you can just text. You need to begin all your texts with our code so that we know it's you. The code is: OpCLT. We have an emergency code as well. This is to be sent only if you believe you or another person is in immediate danger. That code is 911 Rey. You need to erase all messages whenever possible. Is this all clear?"

"Yes sir, all cl—."

Detective Salvino's cellphone barely started to ring and he'd already answered it.

"This is Salvino. Are you sure? The Whole Foods off Soquel Ave. Got it. See you soon."

Officer Rey finished taping the cellphone to her upper thigh. She wore loose pants, flip flops, and a red tank top. Her left eye was swollen, and her upper cheek was split.

"Let's roll Detective," Sophia Rey said.

Detective Salvino dropped Sophia off one block away, on a residential street. She walked to Whole Foods and stood in the front. She looked around and spotted Officer Bailey parked and sitting in a black Honda Civic. He signaled to her to look to her left. She glanced over and saw a man returning his cart near the entrance of the grocery store. She looked back at Officer Bailey to get confirmation and he nodded to her. That was her guy. She slid down the wall of the Whole Foods and sat on the concrete.

"Can you spare some change?" Sophia asked.

Jonas looked down at Sophia and squatted down to her eye level.

"What the hell happened to you?" Jonas said.

"True love sweetheart. You ever heard of it?" said Sophia.

"Where I come from, true love doesn't leave black eyes."

"Well I guess we don't all have your luck," she said.

"I didn't always have this luck."

"Is that so?" Sophia said.

"I used to live on the streets and beg for money every day," Jonas said.

"And what happened? One day God chose to give you a break?"

"You can say that," he said.

"Maybe you can pay if forward, give me a chance," Sophia said.

Jonas stared at her, thoughts circling inside his mind.

"Where you headed anyway," Sophia said.

"Why? You gonna come with me? You don't even know me. What if I was a deranged killer?" Jonas said.

"And what if I am?" Sophia smiled.

Officer Bailey watched from inside the car, his left leg shaking back and forth against the driver side door as he waited to see what would happen. From his vantage point, he saw Jonas kneeling in front of Sophia, blocking his view of her. Then, Jonas stood up and held his hand out to Sophia. She had done it. She was on her way to Freedom House.

Officer Bailey cracked a smile and whispered, "Good luck Rey. Let's bring 'em down."

CHAPTER THIRTY-THREE

She sat in Freedom Park next to the koi pond. It was the first time in a while that Ivy felt confused. Orange, black, and white strokes glided under the surface of the water. The colors blended, and transported her mind back to her mom's apartment, the orange and white floral print couch.

It was a Sunday and the sunlight from the open window was the only brightness that creeped into the apartment. A glimpse out into the world. The sound of children laughing outside was distant and out of reach.

Darleen and Steve had started early that Sunday, around ten in the morning. An empty bottle of vodka was on the living room floor and the cap was missing. Samantha remembered picturing a small ship with sails inside the bottle and imagined herself as the captain, sailing far away, never looking back. Her mother was passed out on the floor and her arm flung over, sending the empty bottle into motion, rolling away and coming to a stop as it hit the wall.

Samantha heard him come out of the bedroom. He swayed back and forth with no shirt on and sloppy, ripped up jeans, the top button popped open from his bulging stomach.

"Darrrleen, git up." Darleen didn't move. Her hair covered her face and she was laid out on her back.

Steve grabbed a half-smoked cigarette out of the ashtray on the coffee table. He searched his pant pockets for a lighter and lit the cigarette. It hung from his mouth hands-free as he stood over Darleen.

"Darrrleen, get your ass up." He kicked her but no response.

Steve kneeled and with his thumb and index finger took the cigarette out of his mouth. He moved the lit side down toward Darleen's arm and pressed it into her forearm.

"What the fuck!" Darleen yelled.

She pulled herself up, holding onto her forearm. Samantha sat on the couch, hugging her knees to her chest and pretending to watch TV.

"What the fuck was that?" she asked.

"I need some food," Steve said.

"I'm not feeling too well baby, can't we—"

Steve grabbed Samantha's mother by her neck and squeezed.

"I said I need some fuckin' food. That's what I need and that's what I'll fuckin' get."

She held his hands at her neck, her veins bulging out of her head and her face bright red. He let go of her and threw her toward the floor. She immediately vomited onto the carpet.

"You disgusting pig," Steve said.

She held herself up with her hands, facing the floor and her hair stuck to her cheek, wet with vomit.

Steve grabbed the back of her hair, holding her hair in his fist. He pushed her face down into the puddle of throw up. "Go ahead, slurp it up."

Ivy heard a muffled sound.

"Ivy? Ivy? Can we talk?" It was Miles.

Ivy's vision became clear as she looked in the pond and saw the koi again, swirling around each other.

"What do you want Miles?"

"I care about you Ivy. I'm sorry if I upset you. Please, we need to stick together."

"I care about you too. I just don't want to ever go back to the outside. I can't. You don't understand."

"I do understand. A lot of us here had it hard on the outside but..." Miles looked down at his hands.

"What?" Ivy asked.

"There's stuff that happens here too. Ivy, I want to show you something tonight when everyone is asleep, but you can't tell anyone that I showed you."

"What is it?"

"I have to show you what's in the Red Room."

Ivy turned and looked at Miles. They stared into each other's eyes.

"Okay," she said.

CHAPTER THIRTY-FOUR

Ivy was feeding the chickens when she first met Sophia Rey. Jonas was introducing her to Miles. As Jonas walked toward Ivy with the woman, Ivy noticed the woman had a black and purple eye. She had been hit by someone and Ivy thought that's probably what led her here.

"Hey Ivy. I'd like you to meet Rey. I met her at the Whole Foods down on Soquel. Rey, this is Ivy."

Ivy reached out her hand and Rey grabbed it with a slight squeeze, holding it about three seconds too long, locking eyes with Ivy. Her touch was strong and purposeful. Ivy saw something in her eyes. Something she hadn't seen in a long time but couldn't explain.

"Hello Ivy, it's a pleasure," said Rey.

"Same."

"Cyrus asked me to bring Rey to you. He said you'd know what she needs next," Jonas said.

"Have you explained the Journey to Freedom to Rey?" Ivy asked.

"Yes. We just discussed that."

"She'll need to meet Skye right away. We also have an afternoon meditation," Ivy said.

"Perfect," said Jonas.

Jonas and Rey turned around and started back to the house.

"Jonas. Rey will need to enter the room of Compassion tomorrow. We have to move fast. Cyrus' orders."

"You got it Ivy," he said.

They disappeared into the house. Miles walked up. He stood next to Ivy, looking out at Freedom Park, scanning everyone working. In a low voice he said, "We still on tonight?"

"Of course," Ivy said.

"I also came over because Cyrus wants to see us," Miles said.

They both sat in front of him, inside his den with candles lit along the walls. Penelope was nearby.

"Ivy, come sit next to me," Cyrus said.

Both Cyrus and Ivy faced Miles as he sat alone in front of them.

"Miles, you are no longer Ivy's mentor. You are being transferred to work in the Red Room."

Miles' eyes widened, fear grew behind them and silent cries reached out through his pupils.

"Ivy no longer needs a mentor. Tonight, half of us will go out into the woods and sleep under the stars one last time. The others who stay back need more time with pain practices and with the room of Compassion."

"When do I start in the Red Room?" Miles voice was low as he looked down at the floor.

"Right away, Miles. You know that," said Cyrus, tilting his head to the left and smirking at Miles.

"Penelope, escort Miles to the Red Room," said Cyrus.

Penelope skipped over to Miles. She locked her left arm into his right arm. "Time to go."

Miles stared at Ivy with a forever goodbye in his eyes. In that window of just a few seconds, his eyes cried out with apologies, begging for forgiveness, and with hope that Ivy would find a way out.

Ivy sat next to Cyrus, side-by-side. He spoke to her but faced forward, without looking at her. His lips moved while his eyes stayed focused on some other place, on his plans for the future of Freedom House.

"Penelope was in the room of Compassion some weeks back when she heard whispers. What do you think she heard Ivy? She heard Miles tell you to get out before it's too late. We cannot let anyone get in the way of the Journey to Freedom. People get jealous. Those are traits that live on the outside and when brought into Freedom House, it strays us from the journey. Do you understand?"

"I understand," Ivy said.

A smile formed across Cyrus' face. His eyes were glazed over with glory as he faced forward and stared into his dream that would soon become a reality.

"That's good to hear Ivy. We will be leaving into the woods soon. It's going to be a night of compassion. A night to be remembered."

Ivy had never been camping in the woods before. She hadn't done a lot of things before Freedom House and as she walked out into Freedom Park she thought about Jody. She thought about Miles and wondered if that was the last time she would ever see him. She liked Miles and as much as she loved Freedom House, something inside made her worry for him. Would she have to force a piece of Miles down her throat like she did Jody? She tried to ignore it but had the feeling that something just wasn't right. There was one thing she knew for sure, she had to get into The Red Room.

"Ivy? Are you ready to go?" Jonas asked.

"Go?" Ivy asked.

"The woods, Ivy. Cyrus wants you all out front. I'll be staying here to lead meditation."

"Right. I'm ready."

While they waited for Cyrus in front of the garden, Penelope, Skye, and two other girls were holding hands to form a circle and danced around. They hummed the same song that Ivy heard those months ago behind the red door. Miles creeped into Ivy's mind, a small faint silhouette reaching for help but disappearing into the depths of her memories.

Ivy watched the girls dance in a circle, Skye's hair fluttering with each jump. The clouds were clear in the sky, but Ivy's mind wasn't. As she thought about Jody and Miles, she could hear the girls humming that song.

"Isn't everything perfect Ivy?" Cyrus walked up.

Ivy forced out, "More than perfect."

"That's my girl."

CHAPTER THIRTY-FIVE

Officer Rey found the perfect spot to hide her cellphone. Detective Salvino was right about hiding it behind the toilet. It wasn't easy since the bathroom in Freedom House had no door and was only a bare doorway, absent of privacy.

"This is where we all shower. We shower together as one. There are no judgements here, just a solitude that will lead us to enlightenment," Jonas said.

Sophia forced a smile. "I need to use the bathroom. Will you excuse me?"

"Cyrus teaches us that we do not have to be ashamed about anything. Everyone at Freedom House does everything and anything in front of each other."

"I'm just finishing up my time of the month, that's all." Sophia moved her eyes down toward her abdomen.

"I know this is very new for you. You'll need to get comfortable in front of everyone, blood or no blood. I'll wait in the hall this time," Jonas said.

He walked out without looking back. Sophia looked around and found tampons and pads under the sink. She grabbed a tampon and sat on the toilet, going through the motions. As she sat on the toilet, her eyes caught the pads again. She grabbed a pad and ripped through the cotton center with her nails.

"You all right in there?" Jonas asked from down the hall.

"Yeah, I'm good. Almost done."

She pulled the tape off her upper thigh as slow as she could but with a sense of urgency. Her eyes squinted as the tape pulled at her skin. She balled up the tape and wrapped toilet paper around it. Her eyes shot at the doorway. She opened the flip phone and sent her first text. Her eyes glanced at the doorway again.

OpCLT got n safe hidin fone

She got down on her knees next to the toilet and placed the phone into the pad and wrapped the pad up. She realized she needed some tape. She looked back at the doorway. She got some tape out of the wadded-up toilet paper from the trash and got back down on her knees to tape the pad to the back of the toilet. She heard footsteps and looked back at the doorway, still vacant. She turned to face the toilet again, the stench of piss filled her nose.

"What are you doing down there?" Jonas asked.

Sophia grabbed the wadded-up toilet paper out of the trash with ease.

She stood up. "Missed the trash," she said, and held up the crumpled toilet paper in her hand.

"Let's head to meditation. Cyrus is out in the woods tonight with some of the others, so I'll be leading it."

Cyrus was the only one who had a tent. The rest of them were to sleep on the ground. Skye was getting a fire started in the center. A thin rug lay in front of Cyrus' tent and he sat on it, staring out at everyone.

"Penelope, it's time to prep the meat," he said.

Penelope took out a large bed of lettuce. She unwrapped it and inside were small cubes of raw, bloody meat. A red puddle soaked the fresh green lettuce. Penelope used her index finger to swirl the blood around and then licked it. Taking out a small container of mixed spices, she dipped each piece of meat and rubbed it through her hands. Once the fire was started, Skye stacked a few rocks on each side of the fire.

"Hey Ivy, can you help me with something?" she asked.

"Of course."

"Come here. Do you see these short stacks I made? We need to find a thin, smooth rock that we can place onto these stacks. It'll be right over the fire and perfect for cooking the meat."

"I can do that," Ivy said.

Walking around the campsite, Ivy searched for the perfect rock slab. Skye walked up to Cyrus and he whispered something in her ear. She looked over at Ivy, catching her eyes for a second. She nodded her head as her ear pressed on Cyrus' words. Cyrus stood up, held his hand out to Skye, and they both entered his tent. She zipped it up.

Ivy continued to look around and made her way behind Cyrus' tent. As she looked along the forest ground, a butterfly fluttered into her line of sight, carrying her gaze up and into the sky. She watched as it moved with grace ever so lightly, reaching high into the sunset. It moved away from her, from them, and from Freedom House.

Whispers from Cyrus' tent caught Ivy's attention. She could see the dimmed shadows of Skye and Cyrus; they were sitting next to each other. Ivy walked to a nearby redwood tree and wrapped her hands around it, using it to hold her breath and keep her still.

"I want her in my tent tonight. She is ready," Cyrus said.

"Yes, she is. I'll be sure she comes to you tonight," Skye said.

"Lovely. You have always been one of my favorites Skye. So perfect in every way."

Through the tent Ivy could see a piece of the dark shadow move up and touch Skye's face.

"Thank you, Cyrus. I am everything I am because of you," Skye said.

"Tonight will be Ivy's time but right now it's your time," he said.

The shadow of his hand moved from Skye's face and up onto her head. It pulled her head down into his lap. A blurred, pulsing movement was masked by the tent. Another butterfly snapped Ivy out of it and like a magnetic force, her eyes followed the flutter of its wings. The butterfly landed on a rock. It was the perfect rock for cooking the meat. Ivy picked it up and the butterfly was still for just a moment then flew away; a forever goodbye.

Ivy walked back and showed Penelope, "I found this rock to cook the meat."

"This'll do. Thanks."

Penelope set the rock onto the fire, the left and right sides were held up with the small rock stacks Skye made earlier.

"Where's Cyrus?" Ivy asked.

"In a yoga session with Skye, the usual. All part of our journey," Penelope said, creating quotations with her fingers as she said yoga session.

Cyrus walked out of the tent, stood in front of it, and stretched his arms over his head. He was naked and his hairy genitals faced Penelope and Ivy's direction, staring at them both.

"Penelope, you ready to cook this meat?" he asked, with a smile that held back laughter.

"Always ready Cy," Penelope said, not one bit surprised by his appearance.

She stood up from the ground, dirt stuck under the crevices of her butt cheeks. She wiped the dirt off using her wet and sticky hands with remnants of raw meat. It created mud streaks across her butt.

The smell of the meat made Ivy sick to her stomach. She couldn't help but think about Jody. She couldn't help but think about Jonas scooping up his own vomit, slurping it down. She thought about Penelope butchering the pig, her fingers always stained with dark red grime as she chopped the food they all ate.

"It smells like heaven Penelope," Cyrus said.

"We are in heaven, aren't we?" Penelope giggled.

Skye walked out clothed from the tent with a calm smile. She gazed at Cyrus with brightness and love. Zipping the tent closed behind him, Cyrus disappeared inside. He came right back out with just his loose pants on, no shoes and no shirt.

"Let's gather around the fire. We will eat soon but first we need to discuss our next steps in our Journey to Freedom," he said.

Gathering around the fire, they all sat in a circle and Skye sat next to Ivy, placing her hand on Ivy's knee.

Cyrus continued, "As you all know, I have been having visions of The Darkness. It's coming for Freedom House, as it usually does when it sees something shining bright. In history, all great endeavors, all great leaders, are faced with a battle of darkness. We must beat this with our practices of compassion, love, and true enlightenment. We must not ever allow darkness to cloud our vision of the truth."

Everyone cheered and shouted reassurances.

"You are all out here tonight because you are the strongest of Freedom House. You are each special. You are perfect. I need you in this journey. It cannot happen without you. Let us feast on this meat and discuss and plan the Ceremony of The Free; a ceremony of celebration that all of Freedom House will participate in."

They raised their spoons to the sky and placed the meat into their mouths. Ivy chewed the meat, switching it from the left side of her mouth to the right side, trying to break it into smaller pieces just to get it down as fast as possible. But it seemed to stay as one big chunk of chewed up bark, each bite squirting juice into the back of her throat. *Was it Jody juice?* Penelope was on her third piece already. Ivy felt a force in the center of her stomach creeping up. She thought about the butterfly fluttering its wings and her jaw chopped with each flutter. The knot in her belly moved up into her chest and hit the back of her throat, burning and sizzling. The vomit pushed up and into her mouth, but she forced her lips to stay shut. The meat marinated in the vomit while she chewed and forced herself to swallow.

"Isn't it so tender?" Skye asked Ivy.

"Delicious," said Ivy, opening her mouth the smallest she possibly could to say the word; the word creeped out from behind her clenched teeth.

"Cyrus wants you to stay with him tonight in his tent. It's really the highest honor." Skye was staring into Ivy's eyes.

Ivy did her best to sound genuine. "I've been waiting."

"I know you have," Skye said.

Sophia Rey had just finished her first pain meditation. She lay in the living space, her hands on her forehead as she attempted to catch her breath. Her eyes watered from the choking. It was similar to some police force training she once had but she was in more shock this time.

"It's exhilarating, right?" Jonas asked.

Sophia thought about Charlotte. She tightened up and put her best poker face on.

"That was amazing," she said through a slight moan.

"I'm glad you are fitting in so fast. We need new members to learn quickly. We will have our Ceremony of The Free soon, so we'll need everyone ready for that."

"What's that?" Sophia said.

"It's when we all become free. It's why we're all here and it's what we've all been waiting for, planning for," said Jonas.

"And what have we been planning for?"

"You'll find out. Since you did so well with pain meditation, you will enter the room of Compassion tonight. I will be your mentor."

"The room of Compassion." Sophia gave a nod.

"The deepest expression of love and compassion," Jonas said. "The core of our practice."

"Penelope has created the perfect feast for our Ceremony of The Free. We will hold this ceremony in a few days and all of Freedom House will partake. It will be our entrance into enlightenment as one. During the ceremony we will eat one last special meal. Penelope has created a sacred sauce that the meat will marinate in for twenty-four hours. I will bless the sauce and all of Freedom House will eat it together. We will show The Darkness that it cannot hurt us. We will complete our journey no matter what tries to get in the way."

They all stood up and held hands around the fire. Lifting their hands above their heads, hands clasped together, they began to move around the fire, a single circle of movement.

Cyrus shouted, "Now we strip ourselves of this darkness!"

They stopped moving around the fire and everyone began to strip their clothes off. Ivy stood still and looked around. She knew what she had to do. They danced around the fire naked, free of restraint. Kneeling next to the fire, Penelope was getting something from her bag. When she turned around to face the bare, fleshy bodies jumping and dancing around, she held raw, bloody meat in her hands. She walked over to Cyrus first and he shouted to everyone again, "This will protect us from the Darkness!"

Penelope's skinny, pale, naked body moved up and down as she rubbed raw meat all over Cyrus' body. He stood with his head pointed high to the sky as she rubbed the wet, bloody meat over his chest and down to his genitals.

"It's almost time Ivy." Skye put her hand out.

"It's time," Jonas said, and put his hand out to Sophia Rey.

Ivy held Skye's hand and walked behind her as she led the way to Cyrus' tent.

Jonas led Sophia down the hall and to the room of Compassion. They stopped and Sophia stared at the door, thinking about Charlotte.

Skye stopped at the tent entrance. She unzipped the tent and looked at Ivy. Ivy stared inside the tent, and the shadows waited patiently for her.

Jonas opened the door and Sophia stared into the room, the fluffy white mattress in the center beckoned them.

Ivy walked into the tent and Skye zipped it close.

Sophia walked in first and Jonas followed. He turned around, looked down the hallway, and then closed the door.

CHAPTER THIRTY-SIX

They never found her. When Charlotte was taken that day, she vanished as if she never existed. It's difficult for memories to survive such a tragedy. Memories of Charlotte seemed to fade away with her disappearance.

The case went cold and the Rey family tried to move forward with living, a single leaf on a branch trying to bring life back again. Sophia watched from a distance as her adolescent years brushed by. Her mother didn't really talk. The eternal despair that lived in her heart seeped out through her eyes. Sophia's dad was the one who continued forward, always looking back and waiting for Sophia and his wife to catch up with him.

Sophia got through high school but was never present, just a body going through the motions. One cold and rainy day after school, she saw her. A glimpse of Charlotte. Sophia was riding on the city bus, the cloudy gray sky passed through the rain drops on the windows. It started as a sprinkle and ended in a storm. Her head rested on the window and her eyes watched as the rain came down and the world passed by.

The bus came to a stop. That's when she saw her. A girl walked onto the bus and everything about her was Charlotte; her long wavy hair and perfectly straight bangs above the eyebrows. She was thin and tall just like Charlotte. More people walked onto the bus and had to stand since all the seats were taken. Sophia could only see the top of the girl's head. The bus made its way to the next stop. Sophia stood up and began to move through the crowd toward the girl, squeezing by each person. A large red purse, a boy with his mom, a skateboard, rolling luggage.

"Excuse me, excuse me, sorry, thanks." She tried to move fast. Sophia raised her arm in the air and yelled, "Charlotte!"

The bus came to its next stop and Sophia grabbed a nearby pole to catch her fall, but her eyes never left the girl. The girl exited off the bus and disappeared onto the street. Sophia made her way to the doors and exited, looking to the left, scanning people, and then to the right, scanning people. Got her. Sophia ran across the street; a car skidded to a stop, the horn was pressed one time, a long howling sound, but Sophia just kept running. She ran through the maze of bodies and locked her eyes on Charlotte. She was almost to her. Her dark hair was almost in reach. Sophia reached out her hand, a gesture of faith, a gesture of resolution. She grabbed Charlotte's shoulder and stopped her. She finally made it; she finally had her.

"Charlotte," Sophia said.

The girl turned around. "I'm sorry, I think you're mistaken. My name's not Charlotte."

The confusion and concern on the girl's face suffocated Sophia. Sophia's mind flashed back to the purple bike on the floor, one wheel spinning all alone. The ice cream truck lullaby and those dark eyes.

"Are you okay?" the girl asked.

"No." Sophia walked away, each step slower than the last. The rain was coming down hard, soaking her hair and showering her face. She stood there, in the middle of the busy street, and let the rain soak her, wishing she could drown right there in it.

She stood there for hours until she finally answered her dad's phone calls. When he picked her up, she opened the car door, sat in the passenger seat, and just stared out the dash, a stench of mildew from her wet clothes.

"Soph, are you okay?" her dad asked.

"I saw her," Sophia sobbed. "I saw her."

"Let's get you home."

Detective Salvino would never forget what he saw that day in Boulder Creek. Six years later and he could still smell the stench of death and hear the deafness of life that lingered in that house. Back then, he was a new detective but had been following the Boulder Creek case since inception.

It began with missing under-age girls and boys. Downtown Santa Cruz was made up of one street, Pacific Ave., and every month new runaways would call it home. Santa Cruz welcomed street dwellers while tourists got a little taste of the hippie town, close enough for fascination but with a distance that kept them cradled in their safe world.

Broken homes spit out kids and teenagers like ash flicked off a cigarette. They were still just kids. Easily manipulated and didn't understand the dangers on the outside. A parent of a runaway could usually find their kid on Pacific Ave. It wasn't difficult to track them down, until that summer. Kids were no longer being found. They were disappearing from the streets. There are things darker than street corners past midnight. When you have addicts looking for their kids, coming into the station, that's when you know there's a real problem.

Detective Salvino took to the streets, questioning the homeless and runaways living along Pacific Ave. and the San Lorenzo River, and he wasn't shy with the dealers who lived down in the Boardwalk flats. Nothing. No leads at first. The first time someone mentioned the "place where they get saved,"

Detective Salvino didn't believe it. He was questioning a young guy, mid-twenties. His hair was oily and spiked to green tips, and dandruff flaked off as he itched his scalp. He wore a jean vest with stapled patches of The Misfits, Agent Orange, and The Sex Pistols across his chest. He sat on the curb and nodded off throughout the conversation, heavy lids for a heavy life.

"I haven't met anyone out here," the kid said.

"We are looking for some missing runaways, under-age. They continue to disappear off these streets. Have you heard anything at all? Do you have any idea where they might be?" Detective Salvino asked.

"I am new here man. I don't know," and as he spoke, his head slowly bobbed down as his eyes closed, then back up as he opened his eyes to the world for a moment.

"Get yourself cleaned up," said Detective Salvino.

A homeless man hobbled over toward the detective. His hair was clumped into one thick single dread, a massive web of stink and dirt. His skin was stained, and his clothes were rags hanging onto any piece of bone they could find.

"It's that place where they get saved. He comes and saves them. Saves them for a better life. A life of ultimate truth, ultimate truth. He saves them." He pointed his finger at the detective and shook it in his face.

"Excuse me sir, what are you talking about? Do you know something about these missing runaways?"

"It's a place to be saved. He comes and saves them."

"Who comes to save them?" the detective asked.

"God. The ultimate truth and life."

Detective Salvino turned around and walked away. A typical day questioning the streets of Santa Cruz. That wouldn't be the last time Salvino heard about the place that saved them. Dreadlock Rags was onto something, but the detective needed more convincing.

He heard it again two days later down at the Boardwalk flats. The flats lay right under The Boardwalk, a tourist magnet that reflected a nice facade of Santa Cruz. Just a block away from the bumper cars, cotton candy, and family thrills, drug dealers sold their own thrills. As long as you didn't cross the street and walk through the parking lot, you would stay a happy tourist, getting back in line for one more ride on The Big Dipper.

Detective Salvino walked up to a chain-linked fence, waist high, and stared at the house. He smoked a Marlboro unfiltered. In less than a second, a Doberman pounced at the fence, standing on its hind legs and barked violently.

A man stood at the front doorway on the porch. He was bald to the skin and wore a tight, white tank top with black Dickie pants.

"Chula, whooot whooot, come!" he said. "Salvino, what brings you down here? Did you come for my wife's pozole?"

"That or maybe something else. How's it going down here Lalo?" Detective Salvino took another drag of his cigarette behind the fence.

"I can't complain. Life is good." Lalo smoothed out his goatee using his thumb and index finger.

"That's a sweet ride you got there," Detective Salvino said pointing his lit cigarette to Lalo's driveway.

"It's a '64. Best year made. Salvino, why don't we cut through the bullshit. What do you need?"

Detective Salvino put his cigarette out. "I just had questions about some missing kids. I'm not trying to step on your toes, but just thought you might've heard something."

Lalo stepped out of his doorway and walked to the top step of his porch. The sunlight brightened his face. A deep scar ran from his right temple down the side of his face and creeped onto his right cheek. He held the buckle on his pants for a moment then walked down the steps and to the fence.

"You talking about those runaways?" Lalo asked.

"I sure am. The thing is, they aren't just running away. Every month more of them go missing. Vanishing from the streets."

"You know me, I don't know anything." Lalo kept eye contact with Detective Salvino.

"They are under-age. Some as young as your daughter."

"There's an officer that keeps creeping down my barrio for no good reason. You know, causing unnecessary tension for mi familia."

"I'll make a call," Detective Salvino said.

"Si, mon. One of my clients has a niece, fifteen-years-old. She's a wild child. Into The Doors and all that trippy shit. She left home and told some of her friends about a place out there in Boulder Creek. The parents spoke to the friends. I heard about the same place when I was downtown last week."

"Boulder Creek. Anything else?" asked the detective.

"That's it."

"Thanks. I'll be sure to make that call as soon as I get back to the station."

Lalo turned around and walked back to the porch. The detective started to walk down the street to his car and heard his name.

"Salvino!" Lalo called.

Detective Salvino walked back, resting his hands on the fence.

"There was one more thing. My client's niece told her friends that she's been saved."

Detective Salvino cracked a small smile and nodded his head at Lalo.

"I'd want my little girl found and then some," Lalo said. His eyebrows pushed down, into his eyes. Hard and filled with heat.

Salvino drove to Boulder Creek, not sure what he was looking for but hoped something would catch his eye. He parked and walked along the cliffs that watched over the ocean. He walked to find the hidden, stopping to listen for sounds of life, but only heard the rumbling of waves hitting the shore. The sun was setting and lit the horizon with a pink and yellow tint that made him stop. He walked down to the beach, a salty mist hit his face and lips. Detective Salvino looked out at the ocean and watched the waves curl up and crash down with both a violence and beauty.

A monarch butterfly flew into his line of sight, coming into focus, and the waves became a distant blur. He watched the butterfly flutter against the pink and yellow clouds and down toward the sand. His eyes followed as the butterfly flew down the shore. He saw something in the distance on the sand. A dark line drawn into it. He walked over and as he got closer more lines came into view. Letters. He stepped back to read it: SAVED.

CHAPTER THIRTY-SEVEN

Officer Rey knew the protocol but made the decision anyway. Jonas closed the door to the Compassion Room. Sophia stood near the door and scanned the room, filing every detail into her mind. The skylight high above the bed, the dark sky watching everything inside the room. The light from the stars, years away, a distance so far that death lies at the other end. She looked down to the bed, a California King with a white, fluffy mattress. Decorative orange and blue pillows contrasted the white. She stared down at the Persian rugs and wondered how the commune earned money for such luxuries. *Stolen, maybe.*

She stared at the bare white walls and then saw the wooden wardrobe against the far-left corner of the room. The wood was carved with an intricate floral pattern. Jonas sat on the bed. He had long, black hair and wore it in a tight ponytail. He was clean shaven with a sharp jawline and dark eyes. He looked at Sophia and with his right hand, patted the bed, gesturing her to sit. Her heart raced and she could feel her palms sweating. She focused on her breath; each inhale thinking about Charlotte, and each exhale thinking about Samantha (it was hard to get used to her as Ivy). She knew what she had to do.

Sophia smiled and said, "What a beautiful room."

"Cyrus says that the Journey to Freedom is made up of three stages. Entrance, Compassion, and Free. Once we complete the Free altogether as one, then we will have completed the journey."

"You mean like enlightenment?" Sophia said.

"I knew I brought you here for a good reason. Everyone at Freedom House is on this journey and together we will all reach enlightenment. We are different than those that live on the outside," he said.

"But we're all *from* the outside," Sophia said.

"Yes, but Cyrus says there are special people on the outside and, like magnets, they attract to one another," Jonas said this in a tone full of logic and seriousness.

Sophia stared into his eyes with a forced seduction that passed as truth. She thought, *Complete brainwash horse shit. How do these people just believe Cyrus' every word and thought?*

"Well, I felt that attraction when I saw you," Sophia said.

"I felt it from you too. I feel it from everyone here at Freedom House. The room of Compassion is all part of our journey to reach enlightenment, to become free. The Compassion stage is a practice of kindness and an opportunity to experience a love that is free of judgement. Something you can never get on the outside."

Sophia knew what this was. She knew and she just thought about Charlotte. She heard the ice cream truck song echoing in her head and saw the police lights flashing along her neighborhood street those years ago.

"Rey, you okay?" Jonas asked.

Sophia blinked and Jonas came into focus, the echo of the ice cream truck song and police lights became a distant memory again, like the stars above her.

"Never been better," she said.

"Well I think Cyrus is going to be happy that you're joining our Journey to Freedom. As your mentor, I will prepare you for The Compassion stage. On a different night, Cyrus will show you the entire stage of Compassion. He does this with every member of Freedom House. I'll show you first because he is very particular."

Ivy walked into the tent, Cyrus followed, and Skye zipped it close. Skye's footsteps faded away as she walked off, the light crunch of leaves under her feet. The inside wasn't as big as it looked on the outside. Rugs were laid out on the floor and a mattress was to the right, sprawled on top was a large, white blanket and four small, orange pillows. To the left side of the tent, two pillows lay on the floor side-by-side, a place for meditation. Cyrus sat on one of the meditation pillows and in his hands, he held raw meat. His hair was pulled out of his face by his bandana. His chest hair was slimy and stuck onto his skin from the meat Penelope had rubbed all over him.

"Sit with me Ivy," he said.

Ivy sat on the pillow next to him and they faced one another. Cyrus placed the meat into his lap and picked up her hands into his and held them with a gentle, almost innocent touch.

"Breathe with me, Ivy. Close your eyes. Inhale deep into your body, into your soul. Take in all your worries. Now exhale those worries out into the world."

They meditated for a while and Ivy's nerves and mind calmed.

"Open your eyes Ivy," Cyrus said.

She opened her eyes and there he was, staring at her with a kindness that she never knew existed.

"Take off your clothes. You also need to be protected from the Darkness."

When all her clothes were off, Cyrus rubbed the meat all over her body. The slimy touch of the meat made Ivy cringe and she held her breath to avoid the smell.

"I am going to kiss you now." Cyrus placed the meat onto the floor.

With his moist hands, he grabbed her face and leaned in. His lips massaged hers and moved at a slow pace. Ivy wondered if this was the meaning of love and compassion. His kiss felt wet and his rough tongue swirled inside her mouth like a koi fish, reaching far down into her throat. She told herself it was all for the Journey to Freedom.

Cyrus stopped. "Now what would you like to do Ivy?" he asked.

She wasn't sure what he was asking but something inside her knew what he wanted the answer to be. Something in his tone reminded her of the room of Compassion.

"Did you enjoy the Compassion room Ivy?" he asked.

"Of course, I did," she couldn't help but stare down at her hands.

"Would you like to practice more love and compassion with me?" he asked, a look of innocence, almost sadness crossed his face.

Ivy could only give a nod.

"That's my girl," Cyrus said and smiled.

CHAPTER THIRTY-EIGHT

Boulder Creek, six years ago.

He stared down at the letters drawn into the sand. SAVED. Detective Salvino looked to the left of the beach. The sun had almost disappeared behind the vast ocean and the waves were crashing harder and closer now. The wind hit his face and he squinted and looked to the right. He looked down into the sand for footprints but instead found the pattern of small, rhythmic hills in the sand, a sign of stillness, lifelessness. He began to walk. He walked and continued to walk in the hopes that he would find the person who wrote this, the person who was saved.

After walking about a mile, he got a call.

"This is Salvino. Repeat that one more time. I'll be right there."

The detective hung up the phone, and out there alone, under the moonlight along the sand he yelled, "FUCK!"

He could run an eight-minute mile normally, but that night he beat that time. It was another half hour to the UC campus. It didn't matter how fast he got there, it was a real-life nightmare and would only get worse. When he drove up, the street was already blocked with yellow tape. He drove right threw it, sirens flaring. College students stood along the street, hugging one another, some of them crying. He had never seen anything like it. 404 Moore Creek Road, just a half mile away from the campus. It was a large, one story house. Three bedrooms, two bathrooms, and a two-car garage. There were cement steps leading to the front door and short, stubby bushes to the left and right that wrapped around the house.

Officer Bailey approached Detective Salvino and said, "Forensics is already inside. It's a death house."

"How many?" Salvino asked.

"Four. All college students," said Bailey.

On this particular night, August 5, 2011, the path leading to the front door was covered in pools of blood. A long, red blood streak at the top step continued into the house, through the open front door and turned around the right corner, disappearing inside. Detective Salvino put on gloves as he examined the blood on the cement steps.

"I don't want anyone inside except for Officer Bailey, the photographer, and forensics. Officer Keaton secure the perimeter. This falls under our jurisdiction so if Investigator Halloway shows, don't take his bullshit."

"You got it," Officer Keaton said, holding onto his belt with both hands.

Salvino walked to the bottom steps of 404 Moore Creek Road. He stared at the puddles of blood on each step as he walked up, carefully maneuvering around each one. At the top step he could see someone was dragged from the step into the house, a blood streak entered the house and brushed along the old carpet, starting in the living room and turning into the dining room. Each step the detective took went at the pace of his breath. He walked into the house, and a few feet into the living room. The front door opened into a large, open space. An old, worn-out, yellow couch was against a wall to the left, the wall that shared the hallway. An olive-green lazy boy was to the right of the couch; it had seen better days. In the middle of the carpet, between the couches and T.V., was the body of Cheryl Bradley, a second year Biology major. From where Detective Salvino stood, he could only make out a body bare of clothing. Blood seeped out from underneath and covered the girl's smooth, cream-colored skin. The light brown carpet was stained around her, a muddy puddle of black and dark red. He looked to his left. There were three visible doors and a hallway to the right, behind the wall that shared the yellow couch.

Bloody fingerprints lined the walls leading to the three doors, someone's gripping hands and fingers attempting to hold onto their life could be made out within the patterns. The blood spanned the entire wall and stopped at the first door. Forensics was already in the first room collecting DNA samples. Inside the room and to the left was a bed with a light teal comforter and a poster hung above the headboard that read:

"You can't wait for inspiration. You have to go after it with a club.

-Jack London."

Closet sliding doors were to the right of the bed and against the opposite wall of the bed was a white desk. The desk was minimalistic with only a small organizer on top that housed colorful pens, pencils, and post it notes. One book lay on the desk, closed, Brave New World by Aldous Huxley. In the far-right corner of the room, to the right of the desk, was a small white shelf. It contained a modest collection of Vinyl records, a row of multicolor slivers waiting to be taken out and played. Underneath the shelf sat a record player on a small dresser. There was only one other poster hanging on the wall, a digital illustration of William Burroughs and a quote at the bottom that read: "We must all face the fact that our leaders are certifiably insane or worse."

The body of Mayra Perez hung halfway over the bed; she was on her back with her feet hanging down and her head still on the pillow. Her rose pink underwear kept her ankles together and her loose, purple tank top was barely visible in the soaked darkness of blood and skin.

"Detective, time of death was about an hour ago."

Salvino nodded his head, staring at the young girl and up at the poster above her headboard.

"It's going to be one of those nights Detective. There are three more."

"Well it's a good thing I'm an insomniac. Did you find anything in this room?" Detective Salvino asked.

"Some hair between the victim's fingers."

"Stab wounds?" asked Detective Salvino.

"Looks like it. And she was the luckiest of them."

"Any sign of the weapon?" The Detective's face was void of any expression as he asked.

"No sir, still looking."

Detective Salvino walked out of the doorway of Mayra Perez's bedroom. He heard the photographer's shutter go off, the flash from the camera lit up the bathroom for a second. Forensics were huddled down on the bathroom tile next to the white porcelain bathtub. The white tiles of the bathroom floor were disrupted by the smear marks of red blood, the brush strokes that signified the end of a life. As the Detective walked closer toward the scene, more details came into view, creating permanent memories in his mind. A memory bank filled with years of violent deaths to haunt his dreams.

The bathroom was decorated with seashells. Ocean blue bath towels hung to the left and their embroidered seashells were hidden behind blood. A hand towel had fallen onto the bloody floor and the remaining towels were almost touching the tiles. The towels had been a false hope for the girl who lay dead in the tub and only provided her with a few seconds of stability before her last breath. The girl was bathing in her own internal liquids. She was Stacy Allen, a third year Psychology major. On the white tile, three small bare footprints could be made out and pointed back toward the door. A female killer and barefoot, what the fuck?

"These footprints seem kind of small for a man," one of the forensic scientists said, as if reading Salvino's mind.

"These are definitely female. No shoes either," Detective Salvino said.

"Not our usual scene boss. It's more than eerie," the crime photographer said, shaking his head.

Detective Salvino backed out of the bathroom doorway. He looked down the hall. At the end of the hallway was a closed door.

"Nothing came up in there?" he asked.

"No sir, just a normal bedroom."

Salvino walked down the hallway. He stopped at the door and could hear the muffled sound of music on the other side. He turned the doorknob as if trying not to wake someone on the other side. As he opened the door, the music became clear. It was Chopin's Nocturne, Op. 9, No. 1. The room was dark, and he could only make out the furniture. Moving his hand onto the wall, he searched for a light switch. Nothing. He placed his right hand to his gun holster and walked in, each step he breathed with intent.

"This is Detective Salvino, is anyone in here?" he said aloud.

He walked to a lamp on a desk and turned it on, but it only lit up the desk with a dimmed light around its perimeter. Barely able to see the room, the lamp only shed light on the dirtiness and grunginess of the room. A large bed unmade. A dresser opposite the bed and sliding glass doors to the backyard. A red curtain was pulled halfway across the doors. The music was coming from a small stereo on the desk. He pressed the stop button, and all went silent. To the left of the sliding doors was the entrance to a bathroom. He turned on the light and the mirror caught his attention. Someone had used their finger to write something in what looked like blood: They've been saved.

Salvino walked out and back to the bathroom.

"I thought you said you checked that room," said the Detective.

"We did. We opened the door and there were no bodies. We had to get started on the rest."

"There was music turned on and blood in the bathroom," Salvino said.

"Sir, there was no music when we went in there."

"Do you think that's the most important part of what I just said?" Salvino asked. "We need photos of the mirror in that bathroom along with samples taken now."

Detective Salvino's phone rang and he walked to the front door.

"Detective Salvino," he answered.

"I'm headed there now. Send backup," the Detective told the officer on the other end of the phone.

"I have to go. Looks like our suspects have been found out in Boulder Creek," Detective Salvino told Forensics, as they kneeled on the bloody bathroom floor.

An anonymous call came into the Santa Cruz Police Department giving the location of a house out in Boulder Creek. The caller had described the four victims of 404 Moore Creek Road. Detective Salvino raced past the beach he had walked along earlier during sunset. Only the moonlight was out, shining a light onto the crashing waves, foaming saltwater brushed onto the shore. There was just highway and only him on it. Outside it was desolate and still. Less than half a mile from the beach was a small road. He made a right onto it and drove through a windy maze that felt never ending.

He passed a green mailbox, number 713, just as the officer over the phone described. And one mile down, there it was, waiting for him: the metal gate. He turned his car off and climbed the gate, jumping down and landing on both feet in a squat position. He stood up as he looked up the pathway to what he'd been searching for and finally found. The only sounds were that of leaves bustling in the wind and his own footsteps. A slowness prevailed all around him.

Walking up the path, he held his gun with two hands and pointed it down toward the ground. To his left and right was the dark abyss of the woods, the depths of trees, bushes, and silence. The dirt path led him to a one-story house on a large plot of land. A tree stood in the front yard to the left and a tire swing creaked back and forth, the movement as short as one last breath. The front door was a lime green color and over the top hung a wooden engraved sign: Home Sweet Home.

Detective Salvino walked up to the green front door, inhaling and exhaling with a gradual ease.

He knocked and said, "This is Detective Salvino with the Santa Cruz Police Department, anyone there?"

He held onto his gun with a firm strength and turned his left ear toward the door, listening for a sign of movement. Nothing. There was only stillness; the isolated silence that swallows the outdoors where people don't belong.

He knocked again with more force, "This is the Santa Cruz Police Department, please open up." Still nothing.

He took his left hand off his gun and placed it on the doorknob. He turned it checking if it was unlocked, hoping what lived behind that door was in fact living. In his twenty years with the police department, he was still not used to that feeling right before opening a door to face the unknown on the other side.

He opened the door with a slow and steady movement, looking intently at every portion of the inside revealed along the way. He released the door and placed his left hand back on his gun, elbows bent slightly. That's when he saw them all and heard the creaking of ropes that turned from their body weight. Inside the living room, bodies hung from the ceiling, all naked. He looked up and caught glimpses of bloodshot bulging eyes and what was left of their tiny squeezed necks, tied like balloons. Each head hung over to the left or right side of each shoulder. There were ten in this room. He still had four more rooms to go, and the rest of the house.

As he moved passed the hanging bodies, he lightly pushed legs aside to get around them. He couldn't help but look up at each breathless face, each soul surrendered to darkness. He stopped at a girl hanging, she looked about twelve-years-old. Her long, blonde hair hung down to her left shoulder. Maybe she had blue eyes, but he couldn't tell behind the bloodshot red that masked over her death stare. As Detective Salvino stared at her, he only heard the creaking sounds from the naked bodies. Salvino's eyes widened as the hanging girl's head lifted, and she reached down, grabbing the detective's face.

The purple veins on her face bulged out and her red eyes saddened, "You came too late. Why detective? You came too late."

Salvino reached for her hands and tried prying them off. He yelled, "I'm sorry."

"Detective, Detective, it's too late." The girl cried then she fell completely silent and still.

No movement, no sound with her head down and hidden from Detective Salvino's view. Her hands fell back to her sides. He breathed heavily and touched his face. He heard a low laughter. He looked at the girl and her head bobbled as she giggled. Her naked body jiggled up and down and she lifted her head up, her neck pulled tightly inward from the rope. Laughing hysterically with her mouth opened wide, she stared into the detective's eyes.

Detective Salvino ran through the living room and into the kitchen. He backed himself against a wall and held his gun up as the girl's laughter became a distant sound. In that moment he received a call on his radio, "Detective Salvino, back up is five minutes away. Over."

Detective Salvino got on his radio, " We're going to need two more on forensics and two photographers, fast. Over."

The noise of the radio filled the lifeless room, "Ten-four. Sending more forensics and photographers, should be another ten minutes. Over."

"We're going to need over ten body bags. Over," the detective said.

"Sir, can you repeat that? Over."

"Send over ten body bags. It's a mass suicide."

With his back against the wall, the detective slid down to the floor, sitting with his gun drawn. He listened. It was silent except for his heavy breaths. He inhaled deeply, his chest rising to his chin. It's just in my head. Fuck. Get a hold of yourself. It's just in my head.

Outside he could hear the sirens in the distance getting closer. He stood up and walked back toward the living room. His eyes locked onto the young girl hanging amongst the rest. All the bodies hung there, spinning the slightest. There was no laughter. There was nothing.

CHAPTER THIRTY-NINE

Sophia Rey lay awake in the Compassion Room. It was early in the morning, around 3 a.m. and Jonas was asleep next to her. She couldn't believe what she had to endure the night before. She thought about the young girls who had to do that too, stripped of their youth but taught to feel otherwise. She lay on her back, eyes open and stared out the skylight at the bright stars. *Is this what happened to Charlotte? To Samantha?*

Officer Rey's eyes filled with tears and a single tear ran down her cheek. She moved her hand slowly to her face and wiped it. She had to check in with Detective Salvino. Staring at Jonas as he slept, she got up from the bed and tiptoed to the door and opened it. She looked down the hallway to check if it was clear. Silence. She went into the bathroom and watched the doorway as she kneeled to get her cellphone hidden behind the toilet. She stayed down on her knees, crouching near the backside of the toilet. She flipped the phone up, keeping her hands low to the floor tiles behind the toilet, and began to type a message to Salvino.

OpCLT im ok it's a sex cul-

"Rey, what are you doing down there?" It was Jonas.

Officer Rey's body froze, and her heart pounded hard into her chest. She set down one edge of the phone onto the tile and carefully rolled it down, the phone touching the tile one millimeter at a time until it was completely flat.

She stood up, facing Jonas who stood in the doorway.

"I was praying," she said.

"Near the toilet?" he asked.

"I was going to the bathroom and started to think about my husband. He beat me in so many places and the bathroom was sometimes the worst of them."

"I'm sorry you had to live that way. You're safe here at Freedom House," he said.

"The wonderful thing about praying is you can pray anywhere. It doesn't matter what you're doing or where you're at," Sophia said.

"Well, almost anywhere," said Jonas.

Sophia looked at him and tilted her head to the right, her eyes waiting for an answer.

"When we die, we can't really pray anymore, right?" he said.

Their conversation was interrupted by a faint humming sound. It was coming from outside the bathroom.

"Do you hear that?" Sophia asked.

Jonas stood still, almost pausing his breathing and only his eyes moved to follow Rey. Sophia walked out of the bathroom and into the hallway, then stopped to listen. It was coming from the red door at the end of the hall. She walked up to the door and placed her left ear to it, both her hands pressed against the door. It was a distant sound of people humming a song, but they sounded far away, deep into the depths of the room that lay behind the door. Not just on the other side, but in some faraway place that was untouchable. *La la la, huuum huuum omm.* Sophia moved her right hand down, onto the doorknob.

She jumped when a hand grabbed her wrist, squeezing it tight.

"You can't go in there," Jonas said.

"Why, what's in there?"

The soft chanting, coming from somewhere inside the room, continued. *La la la, la la la, ommmmm.*

"That's the Red Room. It's a special room that Cyrus assigns members to."

"But what's down there?"

"What makes you think it goes down?" *La la la, la la la, ommmmm.*

"The singing. It's not coming from right behind the door. It sounds like the room goes downstairs," said Rey.

"I don't hear anything," said Jonas, with a closed mouth smile and a glare in his eyes.

"Must have been in my head. I'm still a bit uneasy."

"I think so. Let's head back to the room and try to get a couple hours of rest before morning chores," Jonas said.

They went inside the room of Compassion. Jonas opened the door and walked in first. Rey was behind him. She heard the humming again and stopped at the doorway. Turning back to look at the door to the Red Room, her eyes locked onto it and she saw Charlotte's purple bike, alone on the street. She blinked and the red door came into focus. She knew she had to find out what was down there.

CHAPTER FORTY

Ivy woke up in the tent. Cyrus was asleep, but his naked, clammy body lay against hers. His skin and body parts were sticking to hers. She had dreamed of the Compassion stage with Cyrus for so long, but lying there in his tent the next morning, Ivy only felt one thing: dirty and shameful. It hurt more than the night with Miles. It also went all night long. Ivy told Cyrus she was tired and ready to go to sleep, but he insisted that if they didn't continue, the Darkness would arrive sooner.

She knew she couldn't just leave the tent. She knew there was nobody there for her to talk to except Miles, but now Miles was in the Red Room and she felt it was all her fault. Lying there next to Cyrus she tried to breathe as slow as possible. All she wanted was to get dressed and get out of the tent. It smelled of plastic tarp and sweat.

Moving as slow as she could, Ivy slid her body away from his, her skin peeling off his sticky thighs. She sat up and felt something wet underneath her. Looking down and opening her legs, she could see blood and felt a stinging sensation inside of her. She touched in between her legs and under, near her butt. It was coming from inside her butt. She looked back at Cyrus and he was in a deep sleep, his chest moved at a steady pace from his breath. Using the bed sheet, she wiped the blood. She stood up and moved slowly toward her clothes on the ground, but it was difficult to walk. Her insides hurt.

Bending down gently, she picked up her underwear from the floor. She tried to lift her right leg up but could barely get it a couple inches off the ground. She almost fell over.

"Do you need help with that?" Cyrus asked.

Ivy dropped her panties back onto the floor. Her back faced him and she stared at the green canvas walls of the tent, keeping her from the outside world.

She didn't turn around when she spoke but said, "I need to help the girls with breakfast."

"I think they have it handled," said Cyrus.

Ivy's heart began to race, and she just wanted to be free from the sour smell of the tent. There was no one to help her and nowhere to go.

"I'm kind of hungry and want to help get breakfast started," she said, trying to sound casual.

"If you're hungry, I have something special for you. You are beautiful Ivy. One of my favorites here at Freedom House."

She turned around to face him as he lay on the mattress. His dirty blonde hair hung down in front of his face, oily from the sweat the night before. His naked body lay out and he stared into her eyes, not asking her but telling her to come to him. What could she do? He was bigger and stronger. In that moment she felt something she never imagined she would ever feel. She wanted to go home. She wanted to sit on that dirty, orange couch in her living room apartment. She wanted to see her mother even if she was stumbling around with her glass of vodka. But she had been gone for so long, she couldn't just leave Freedom House. She couldn't just leave Cyrus. What would happen? What if she was never found or never seen again? And worse, what if her mother didn't want her anymore?

"Ivy, I need you. Freedom House needs you," Cyrus said, with a slight demand in his tone.

She walked over to him and laid with him. She could hear the birds chirping high up towards the bright sky. She tried to free her mind by thinking about her life on the outside, trying to ignore everything else inside the tent. She thought about Slim Steve and her days hanging out on Pacific Ave. She thought about how simple her life was when she got to watch T.V. in her living room back home. Miles tried to warn her but now he was gone, into the depths of the Red Room. She needed to find someone else to help her. This is what she thought about as she waited until Cyrus was done with her.

CHAPTER FORTY-ONE

That day in Boulder Creek, years ago, changed Detective Salvino. There were thirty-six bodies discovered, fifteen were young boys and girls. It was a mass suicide, if you can even call it that for the kids. It was more of a brain- washed suicide. Rumors circulated that there was one male survivor, but it was never confirmed. After Santa Cruz PD searched the house, they found stacks of literature and videos by the Boulder Creek leader. They called their cult Kingdom of Light and their leader, Apollo. He claimed that all who entered and devoted their lives to the Kingdom of Light, would be truly saved. Once saved, they would have their ticket to the kingdom of all light, of all love, and of all happiness.

Further investigation into Apollo revealed that his true name was William Thatcher, also known as Willy Thatch in The Tenderloin, the San Francisco neighborhood he once called home. He was raised in a shithole apartment above a liquor store on the corner of Leavenworth and O'Farrell. His mother was a prostitute and he never had or knew of a father. Willy started off by robbing stores and neighbors then moved to running drugs on the streets. It was never a dull moment for business in the Tenderloin, the streets bred homeless zombies like a flesh-eating virus, deteriorating the skin down to raw meat and bones.

Willy Thatch could move any drug and fast until a new drug lord showed up and began to clean house. Willy left the Tenderloin at age twenty-eight, moving onto bigger and better things in Santa Cruz, CA. He had heard of the university and the hippie, free life culture it induced. With his many professional street connections on the outside, he knew he'd be of value to the students who majored in expanding their mind through experimentation. He could make some money, find free love liberals to crash with, and probably get laid throughout the process. It was a win-win for Willy Thatch, so he began his journey and hitch-hiked from San Francisco to Santa Cruz. And Santa Cruz didn't know what was about to hit them.

Willy was dropped off on Pacific Ave. at Bonesio Liquor Store. He had his red hiking backpack stuffed with clothes and a college student's dream drug store, a store that could build reputations, produce the addicts of the world, and end the lives of a few unlucky first time tryers, those horror stories you hear about on the news.

This Just In: A first year UC Santa Cruz student was found dead this morning when her roommate went to wake her and she didn't respond. The student lived in the dorms on campus at Oakes College. She was a Film major and had already made many friends here at Oakes. Traces of heroin and cocaine were found in her system and her death was ruled an overdose. Her family and friends said she's never been known to do drugs and police believe it was her first time experimenting. A tragedy that has ended such a short and young life. Reporting to you from the University of California, Santa Cruz. I'm Ashley Landis.

Willy went inside Bonesio Liquor Store, a small cramped space that reeked of cigarettes and that had the sole purpose of selling liquor to the local drunks and to the lucky college students who were fortunate enough to pay for a fake I.D. He walked in and bought a pack of unfiltered Camels and a twelve oz bottle of Jack.

As he paid, the cashier said, "Never seen you around here."

"I could be a college student," Willy said.

"You're too old. There's no loitering outside my store either."

"I'm not looking for any trouble man," said Willy.

"No, but you look like trouble."

"Maybe trouble finds you," Willy said.

"Maybe." The cashier pushed the pack of Camels toward Willy. "6.75."

Willy put a ten-dollar bill on the counter.

"Keep the change," he said, and he walked out.

He stood against the front wall of the liquor store and took out a cigarette, lit it, and turned the cap on the Jack; the feeling of the cap cracking open brought the same feeling of relief to him every time. He took a swig.

"Excuse me sir?" It was a young man, blond with a clean haircut, and wearing a red Adidas shirt with cargo shorts. His shoes were white and clean. Willy looked up as he leaned against the wall, one foot up against the wall and the other on the ground.

"Do you think you can buy me a bottle? I have the cash here and you can keep the change." He was polite and held the cash in his hand for Willy to see.

"The owner's a real dick," Willy said, taking a drag of his cigarette and blowing it into the boy's direction.

"So, no then?" the boy asked.

"That's a hard no. But I do have something you might like better," said Willy, his dirty blond hair to his shoulders clumped together from not washing it for days.

"I don't smoke cigarettes," the boy responded.

"Well that's good because I'm not talking about cigarettes. I have something that will show you the world in an entirely different way. It will save you from a hangover or all the other bullshit drinking causes," Willy said.

"But you're drinking," the boy chuckled.

"Exactly. And look at me," Willy said.

"So, what is it?" The boy gave him a suspicious look, ready to be unimpressed.

"You got a house we can go to?" asked Willy.

"Actually yeah, I'm headed to a party at a friend's house. Was coming here to do a liquor run but if you have something better, then, hey I'm down. My friends are always down too," the boy said.

"Right on," said Willy.

"How do I know you're for real though?" the boy asked.

Willy looked to the left and right. He scouted the street and then reached into his pocket. He pulled his hand back up and onto his jeans at his waist with his hand closed like a fist.

"I'm cool if you're cool." Willy put his fist out towards the boy and the boy naturally went in for a sly handshake. The boy could feel Willy open his hand and pass a plastic bag into his palm. Keeping his fist closed, the boy looked down at his hand then opened it the slightest to see what it was. A gram of coke.

"I'm definitely cool," the boy said. Willy nodded his head.

"We can walk to the party from here."

And together, they walked down Broadway. That's all it took. One friend, one party, and one Willy Thatcher. From that point on, Willy Thatch became Apollo and built the Kingdom of Light. And just like that, six months later, thirty-six people committed a mass suicide in the belief that he was their ticket to the Kingdom.

CHAPTER FORTY-TWO

When they returned to Freedom House, Ivy was a different girl. Her youth had stayed trapped back there in the woods, inside that tent to never be found again. She wanted to find Miles. She was sitting in Freedom Park in the only place that could clear her mind, the koi pond, but the pond looked different too. The rocks around the edge of the water seemed darker as they disappeared down into the depths. The koi seemed more helpless and trapped than she remembered. She watched as their orange and white colors, like the splatter of paint, spun around under water, twisting and turning along one another. They were trying to go somewhere but trapped in their own world.

"Hey Ivy." Jonas walked over with Rey. Rey stared into Ivy's eyes without breaking eye contact. Ivy felt a sense of safety around her but didn't know why.

"Hey," Ivy said.

"How was sleeping under the stars?" Jonas asked.

Ivy looked away from Rey and back at the koi swimming in circles.

"It was great," she said.

"Did Cyrus start planning for the Ceremony of the Free? We've been working hard over here. Rey experienced the room of Compassion. Everything's coming along," he said.

Ivy made eye contact with Rey again. Her eyes were different than anyone else's at Freedom House. There lived a longing and a purpose that showed through them and rooted in her soul. Their eyes stayed locked together.

"Yes, we started planning for it as well. Everything *is* coming along," said Ivy.

"That's great. Well, I came over here to see if you could show Rey how to feed the animals. I have to meet with Cyrus," said Jonas.

"Of course, no problem."

"Thanks Ivy. Rey, you're in good hands. I'll see you both in afternoon meditation."

"Thanks Jonas," Rey said.

He walked away, through the doorway that led to Cyrus, a doorway where all freedom was gone.

"So, how do you like it here so far?" Ivy asked Rey as they walked away from the koi pond, down the stoned path toward the animals.

There was a light wind that started to slow dance with the leaves above their heads and the sun was high in the sky. It almost felt like everything was going to be fine, but masked over this beautiful day was a darkness. Cyrus was right, there was a darkness upon them, but it wasn't the darkness he spoke of, it was something else.

"It's been pretty good. Jonas has been a great mentor so far. What about you?" Rey asked.

Her hair was pulled back into a French braid and her age hinted through the soft wrinkles on her forehead and under her almond brown eyes. She kept trying to catch Ivy's eyes as they spoke, the same way you can feel someone's stare from far away, a soft whisper into your ear to look their way.

"Ivy? You okay?" Rey asked again.

"Yeah, I'm just a little tired from our camping trip."

"Oh yes, how was that?"

Ivy tried in that moment to fake joyfulness but there was nothing left inside of her to pretend. It had all been taken from her in that tent. Her eyes looked down into the dirt path as they approached the fence that confined the chickens, pigs, and peacocks.

"Good." That's all she could muster up.

Sophia Rey looked around Freedom Park with a calmness that came off as natural. She checked to be sure there was nobody nearby to hear them.

She lowered her voice and said, "Ivy, what's your real name?"

Ivy's face turned bright red, a heat that rushed so fast she could feel the temperature rise out of her skin, into the air all around her. She tried to force the tears from filling her eyes but for some reason couldn't control herself. Turning her back to Rey, she wiped the tears that fell down her cheeks. She didn't know what to say and wasn't sure why Rey was asking her what her real name was.

"Is your name Samantha Watson? I am here to help you," Sophia whispered.

Ivy's instinct was to play dumb. The fear that lived inside of her forced her to say, "I'm not sure what you're talking about. I don't need help." She wiped away more tears from her cheeks.

"Samantha, you're in danger. Very serious danger. I am here to help you, to get you out of this place. Cyrus is extremely sick and everyone here at Freedom House is going to get hurt unless something is done about it."

Ivy was catching each breath to keep from making a sound as she cried, her back still to Rey.

"You can't help us. It's too late," Ivy said.

"It's never too late Samantha. That's what he wants you to think. People survive worse things than this."

"Maybe I don't want to survive to remember this. Who are you anyway? Why were you sent here?"

"I can explain but we cannot bring attention to ourselves. Let's feed the animals and I'll explain. Is that okay?" Rey asked.

Was this really happening? Did Ivy have a chance to get out of Freedom House? What if someone found out? What would happen to them?

In that instant, Ivy broke down like the child she was and said, "I'm scared, I just want to go home."

"I know you do. You have to follow my instructions. You need to stop crying and we must feed these animals. Sound good?"

Ivy inhaled a deep breath and exhaled. She wiped her cheeks and turned around to face Rey, "Okay, that sounds good."

"Great. My name is Detective Sophia Rey and I'm going to get you out of here."

CHAPTER FORTY-THREE

That sunny day in the middle of Freedom Park, as they fed the animals, Officer Rey told Ivy as much as she could. She told Ivy that her mother was looking for her. She told her they had been looking for her for months. Then she told Ivy that Freedom House was called a cult and that cults could be dangerous, even deadly. She explained how Cyrus was brainwashing everyone at Freedom House and that if Ivy stayed it would be her death sentence. She also explained that she had to try and save the people of Freedom House before something horrible happened. At the end of all this, Sophia asked Ivy for help.

"I'm not sure how I can help but I'll try. There is something. The Red Room," Ivy said.

"The red door that's always locked?" Sophia asked.

"Yeah. That's where they send members who haven't obeyed their rules. My mentor, Miles, he was sent there, about a week ago. I haven't seen him. A girl was sent there a month ago, Jody. Cyrus said she sacrificed herself. And we—we ate her."

Sophia's almond brown eyes widened as she placed her hand over her mouth. Her head shook back and forth at the pace of a floating feather.

"My God. Have you've been inside that room?" Sophia asked.

"No, never. And I didn't know what I was eating until it was... all chewed up in my mouth."

"It's going to be okay. I'm here now," Sophia said.

"I've never been in that room but I have to get in. I have to find Miles."

"It might be too dangerous for you to go in Samantha. I can get in and–"

"I will help you but only if I can go too. I owe it to Miles. He tried to tell me about this place, and I didn't listen at the time. He's in there because of me." Tears crept into Ivy's eyes but she swallowed, hoping that would keep them down.

"Alright then," Sophia said and stared into Ivy's eyes.

"So when do you we go?" Ivy asked.

"Do you know who has the key?"

"Cyrus has one. Penelope, the chef, has one too," Ivy said.

"It'll be easier to get it from Penelope. Where does she keep it?"

"I can get it. I'll handle Penelope," Ivy said.

"Okay. You get the key tonight and we'll go into the Red Room tomorrow night. Are you sure you can get it without getting caught?" Sophia asked.

"I'm sure."

She had heard of females mentoring other females. She heard that Skye and Penelope went into the Compassion Room more than once together, so she knew it was possible. She waited until it was near bedtime. Penelope was in the kitchen in her usual white apron, nothing underneath except her panties. One by one, she was sharpening her knives.

"Hey Penelope," said Ivy, giving her an innocent smile.

"Ivy, how goes?" she asked, as she sharpened a large cutting knife. The high pitch singing sound of each side being sharpened was in the background as they spoke.

"Pretty good. That camping trip was amazing, don't you think?" Ivy asked.

"It was more than amazing. My insides felt so free. I bet you feel great after spending the night with Cyrus. That's always so exciting. How'd it go?" Penelope stopped sharpening her knife, placing it down onto the counter but still held onto the handle, and looked at Ivy.

"Actually, he talked a lot about you," Ivy said, keeping eye contact with Penelope.

Her expression softened, content rippled down her face. "He did?"

"Oh yes, you're really one of his favorites. He told me I should consider asking you to be my mentor. My mentor in the Compassion Room. He said if you agree then he would be sure to spend the night with both of us." Ivy spoke every word clear and concise.

A seductive smile appeared on Penelope's face. "Well, I'm not sure what we're waiting for. When Cyrus suggests something, we do it."

Ivy mirrored Penelope's smile back at her.

"Let me finish up here and I'll meet you," Penelope said.

She turned around and bent far down to put away a large pot into a bottom cabinet, her white apron exposed her back and butt cheeks, the string tied around her waist.

Ivy waited on the fluffy, white comforter and held an orange pillow adorned with silver and blue sequins. She stared at each tiny orifice with thread running in and out and moved the pillow back and forth, watching the reflection of the sequins against the wall. Her thigh was being lightly brushed by something, giving her an instant tickle that had to be scratched. Flipping the pillow over, she realized it was the pillow's tag. It read: Pottery Barn.

Are you fucking kidding me? The load of bullshit that this place smelt of, that she was starting to see through, made her nauseous, that familiar warm, burning of vomit rose into her throat. The door opened abruptly.

Closing the door behind her, Penelope walked in. She walked over to Ivy, sitting on the bed, and stood in front of her. She moved her leg in between Ivy's knees, her apron right in front of Ivy's face. She placed her hands behind her back and fiddled for a moment, then her apron dropped to the floor and now her belly button was in front of Ivy's face. She caressed Ivy's hair with her small, delicate hand. With her fingers, she grabbed Ivy's hair into her fist, pulled her head back to face her and leaned over Ivy to meet her eyes and asked, "Are you ready to truly feel free?"

After her night with Penelope, there was no doubt in Ivy that she had to escape Freedom House. Penelope was as rough and brutal as Cyrus. The disturbing glee in Penelope's eyes as she inflicted pain was far beyond human, it was animalistic. Ivy waited until Penelope fell asleep. Her apron was still on the floor where she had dropped it. Ivy got down on the floor and stayed there while she picked up the apron and felt inside the front pocket. Bingo. Pulling out her hand, there lay the key to the Red Room on her palm, simple and silver but the one thing that would help her get freedom. The one thing that would help Miles get freedom.

Ivy hid it in her underwear. She only hoped Penelope wouldn't immediately check her apron pocket when she woke up. *Please God, don't let her check.* Ivy got back into bed, slowly moving her legs under the white blanket. She stared up at the skylight and looked at the night sky, the stars seemed closer, brighter, and she couldn't help but smile. She tried to fall asleep but was too anxious, so she just lay there looking up into the dark sky with all her hopes, all her fears, and all her freedom in the hands of Detective Sophia Rey.

CHAPTER FORTY-FOUR

They met to feed the animals the next day.

"Good morning Ivy."

"Good morning…" Ivy paused, "Rey." She had to force the word detective back down her throat before it rolled off her tongue and out of her mouth into Freedom Park.

"Shall we load these buckets for the chickens?" Ivy asked.

"Of course," Sophia said.

They bent down to the dirt and kneeled there. In her palm, Ivy had the key ready for Sophia. Ivy's palms were clammy and moist, the sweat on her face made her hair stick to her skin, shiny and wet. She placed the key down onto the ground, next to the bucket. Sophia grabbed it and placed it into her bikini top. There was no change in her facial expression. Looking at Ivy, she moved her lips, but no sound came out. Her mouth silently said the words, "good job."

Penelope had not looked in her pocket that morning. She got up early without a word and went out to start breakfast.

It just meant that they had to get into the Red Room tonight because the longer they waited, the longer Penelope had to discover the key missing.

The rest of the morning and afternoon, Freedom House was more alive than ever. Everyone was following Cyrus' orders which meant non-stop preparations for the Ceremony of the Free. He had set the ceremony for the next day. Penelope was in the kitchen handling pounds of raw meat, seasoning it, and getting ready to cook it. She used her bare hands and wiped the sweat from her forehead using her wet hands. Thin, slimy remnants of raw meat streaked across her forehead. A sour, spoiled stench filled the house.

Pain meditation and pain yoga were going on all day and they were required to continuously practice and endure the pain in order to be fully ready for the Ceremony of the Free. Cyrus was leading the pain meditation, and Ivy sat there, waiting for the next meditation session to begin. Cyrus was wearing white, loose, flowing pants and a white vest over his bare chest. His silky, long hair was straight and he wore an embroidered band around his head. There were about twenty people sitting around him in a large circle, with him in the center as always.

"Something exciting is coming tomorrow," Cyrus said. Something that will change all our lives. It's the reason you all came here to Freedom House. It's what you have been searching for your entire lives, whether you know it or not. It's the reason we are born. Tomorrow, we will all become free and reach total enlightenment as one. Today, we must continue with our pain meditation practices in order to truly appreciate what's coming tomorrow. We must transcend the darkness that is coming."

And with that, Ivy experienced her last pain meditation at Freedom House.

They waited until everyone was asleep. Ivy met Officer Rey in the bathroom, just feet away from the Red Room, a place of mystery that clawed at their minds, always resting there in their hearts.

"Are you ready for this?" Sophia asked.

"More than ready," Ivy said.

"Here's what we're going to do. I will lead the way. You must stay close behind me. I want you to take this," she said and handed Ivy the small phone.

"You have contact with the outside?" Ivy asked, realizing how stupid it sounded after it came out.

"Yes. I want you to carry this. If anything happens, if we get caught, I need you to just run and call the one number saved in that phone."

"Who is it?" Ivy asked.

"My boss, Detective Emilio Salvino. He knows about everything that's happening here. He knows who you are too. If anything happens, you call that number."

"Why can't we just call now?" Ivy asked.

"I haven't witnessed anything illegal. We have to get the timing perfect if we want to put a stop to this. Trust me. Follow my instructions."

Ivy nodded. Officer Rey turned toward the bathroom doorway and began to walk to the hallway and Ivy followed right behind her. Her heart throbbed down to her knees and shot to her toes. The pit of her stomach felt heavy and turned with every step she took. The hallway was dark, and the house was quiet except for light snores from the living room and the faint creaks of Sophia and Ivy's footsteps against the floorboards. Sophia took out the key and inched towards the doorknob, the sound of the key entering the lock seemed to echo in the hall. Slowly turning the key, they both heard the click. Sophia opened the door and it wasn't a room they were looking into but a cement staircase leading down underground. They walked in and stood at the top of the stairs and Ivy closed and locked the door behind them.

Officer Rey turned to Samantha and said, "Remember, if anything happens, you run and call."

CHAPTER FORTY-FIVE

The cement steps led down into a long, narrow corridor, an underground tunnel that led to something unknown but soon in their reach. The corridor was dark and cold but flickering lights came from bulbs above them every few feet, providing a dim lit path as they walked. They walked at a pace to not be heard and listened for any sounds, but there was nothing. Not yet.

It seemed like they walked for five minutes down the straight corridor before reaching a turn, and when they made that turn, there was more corridor, down into the depths of flickering lights and silence. So, they walked. Left turn, straight down, another left turn and straight down, and a right turn. This is where the lights stopped and the tunnel led into darkness, swallowed by pitch black darkness.

Sophia turned around to face Samantha and whispered, "Hold my hand. We need to walk very slow. I will lead the way, okay?"

Samantha nodded her head once and grabbed Sophia's hand, squeezing it without meaning to. She turned to look behind them, the last of the flickering lights, the last of what was visible. In front of them was a darkness so black, they couldn't see their arms. The type of darkness that a person disappears inside of, blends in with, becomes part of, becomes nothing and there is nothing except the dark. The only sound was that of their shuffling feet and small, short breaths. The fear that lived in them was louder than their movement, and they moved an inch, then paused until they moved another inch.

Ivy always thought that not being able to see what's ahead, not knowing what's about to come out in darkness, would be the worst thing to ever experience, but soon she'd be proven wrong. There are some things that you never want to see; that you wish you could unsee and that make the darkness a comforting place. They walked with the movement of the blind and stopped when they both heard the same noise. It was a groaning sound in the far away distance, a cry maybe, like someone in exhausting pain close to giving up but still with a sliver of hope that they might be heard. Sophia and Samantha were their sliver. The darkness around them reverberated with the echoed cries.

Ivy squeezed Sophia's hand and whispered, "I'm scared."

Sophia stopped walking and Ivy knew she turned around only because she could feel her breath near her ear as she whispered back in total darkness, "I am too but we are the only hope to save them, to save Miles."

"What if I can't? What if we never get out of here?" Ivy asked and began to cry.

Sophia placed her hands onto Ivy's shoulders with a gentle touch, like that of a mother, and said, "If you don't try, you won't get out and you will end up in this dark place forever."

Down in the depths and darkness of the Red Room, she hugged Samantha like someone she loved dearly. The moaning cries in the distance echoed around them as they hugged.

"Are you good?" Sophia asked.

"I'm good."

Ivy felt for her hand and held it. They walked toward the cry and something brushed against their feet, scurrying by and sending chills up their legs, through their spines and over their necks. That's when they heard it. Little claws scratched at the ground and squeaking noises passed beneath them. Sophia and Samantha both froze and just stood in the dark waiting for the rats to pass by.

CHAPTER FORTY-SIX

Penelope soaked the small towel in the bath bubbles, moving it down into the water, massaging it between her hands. She pulled it out and ran it across Cyrus' back. They both sat in the tub in the bathroom inside the Compassion Room. She moved the towel in slow motions along his back, creating soap bubble streaks along his bronze skin. His hair was pulled up into a dry bun at the top of his head. His neck muscles bulged out as his head hung down against his chest. His eyes were closed.

"Thank you for all you do," Penelope said, "You are my reason for living. Freedom House is why I want to live. I am so grateful to have found this place and you."

"Mmmmmm," Cyrus moaned a sound of relaxation, confirming he was hearing her voice but not necessarily listening.

Penelope moved the towel back into the water and moved it onto his back, squeezing the warm water over his shoulders.

"I am more than ready for the Ceremony of the Free. I've been waiting so long for this. I think we are all ready."

Cyrus spoke as he hung his head down with his eyes closed, "Penelope, I knew you were always a very special girl. Always my favorite."

Penelope smiled as she washed his arms. "Well, Ivy told me what your wishes were, so I followed them."

Cyrus' head hung down to his chest as she massaged the soap along his arms and shoulders. His eyes opened abruptly. His right hand lifted out of the water and grabbed Penelope's hand, massaging his left arm, and he stopped her. "What wishes?"

She giggled and touched his back with her hand.

"What do you find so funny?" Cyrus asked, there was no inflection in his tone, just a sternness that shut her up.

"Get out of the tub," he said.

Penelope got out and grabbed a towel, holding it up to her mouth while she stared at Cyrus. He stood up in the bathtub and stared at her.

"What wishes?" he asked with a look of concern that she saw for the first time ever.

"Ivy, she said you wanted me to mentor her in the Compassion Room and that you'd spend the night with both of us together. I was happy to do it for our journey."

As Penelope saw Cyrus' expression transform from concern to anger, her voice faded out as she spoke. They both just stood there, in the bright white bathroom. Cyrus stood in the tub facing Penelope as she hugged the towel.

"Well, it seems we may have a problem," Cyrus said.

"So it does," said Penelope. "What do you need me to do?"

"Wake Ivy. Bring her to me. It just might be her time to see the Red Room," Cyrus said.

Penelope stepped closer, her shins against the bathtub and the tub was the only thing between them. She dropped the towel to the floor and wrapped her arms around Cyrus' naked waist.

"Please forgive me. I should've come to you first to confirm what she told me."

"I can forgive you," Cyrus placed his hand onto Penelope's head and pushed it down.

She wanted his forgiveness and she knew what she needed to do to get it. Cyrus stood in the bathtub and held her bobbing head as he looked at himself in the mirror, his blue eyes lost in a darkness far away, and he smiled as he watched his reflection.

CHAPTER FORTY-SEVEN

Penelope walked out into the hallway. The house was quiet and still as everyone slept. She went into the living room and looked down at the people, deep in their slumber. Scanning the room, she looked for Ivy. Her heart dropped into the pit of her stomach. Ivy was not there.

Penelope ran outside into Freedom Park. The moonlight hung over her and the sounds of an owl could be heard in the distance. The chickens and pigs were quiet and there was no activity out there except the flowing dance of the leaves above her head. She went to the koi pond but only an empty bench watched over the fish while leaves rolled by.

She ran down the stone path to Cyrus' room, but she found herself standing in an emptiness, the sound of her beating heart filling her eardrums with dread. She ran back to the house to look in all the rooms, but she knew Ivy would not be found there. She looked anyway, a lie to herself that this may just be a nightmare that she'll wake from.

Penelope walked into the Compassion Room.

"Where is Ivy?" Cyrus asked, lying on the bed with his legs crossed and hands on his stomach.

"I don't know. I looked everywhere and I couldn't find her."

"There's only one more place she could be, isn't there?" Cyrus said.

He stood up and walked over to Penelope, just a few inches from her face. He grabbed her neck and squeezed it between his fingers. Penelope's face turned red and she stared at Cyrus with a smile, her face shook from his grip.

"We cannot let her get away. She belongs to Freedom House," he said. He released her neck and she continued to smile.

Cyrus walked out of the room and stood in front of the Red Room door. Penelope followed him.

"Unlock it," Cyrus said.

Penelope reached into her apron pocket and felt the emptiness at the bottom of the pocket seams. She checked the other pocket and felt Cyrus' eyes digging into her mind, like the claws of a vicious tiger tearing into the flesh of its victim to get a taste of fresh, raw meat. She looked up at him.

"It's not here. I don't understand. I always keep—"

With full force, Cyrus slapped her across her left cheek, and she spun around and fell to the ground. He took his key from his pocket and unlocked the Red Room door and stared down into the stairway. Cyrus' face was hardened with anger but there was glee in his eyes as he imagined what he was going to do to Ivy when he found her, an opportunity for him to play and teach her a lesson.

"I'm sorry Cyrus. I'll go with you and—"

Cyrus interrupted Penelope, "Get me Jonas. I don't need you."

Penelope's eyes filled with hurt, but she did as commanded. She walked to the living room and shook Jonas.

"What time is it?" He yawned and stretched out his arms.

"Cyrus is asking for you. It's an emergency," Penelope said in a low voice as to not wake the others.

Jonas stood up and followed her. He saw Cyrus standing in front of the Red Room, facing the stairwell that led down. Cyrus did not turn to look at Jonas. His eyes stayed locked on the stairwell leading into his next journey that would quench his thirst. Jonas stood next to him and waited.

Cyrus continued to look down and said, "Jonas, we have a little problem. Ivy is missing along with Penelope's key to the Red Room. Do you know anything about this?"

"No." Jonas' eyes moved back and forth as his thoughts connected, then he ran back to the living room and looked at all the members sleeping. He went back to Cyrus.

"Rey is missing too."

Cyrus now turned and looked at Jonas.

With a calmness in his voice, Cyrus said, "Well, I guess we know what that means. We must show them how important the journey is because it's clear they don't understand."

And with that, Cyrus walked with a grace down the stairs, not rushing and not running. Jonas followed and as he closed the door behind him, Penelope stood there looking down at them, wishing Cyrus needed her like he needed Jonas.

CHAPTER FORTY-EIGHT

They finally saw a dim light around a corner. Sophia and Samantha moved faster toward the end of the corridor. They turned right and at the end of the hall was an open space. The moaning voice grew louder and was coming from this open space. They could see a large, wooden table in the center, and on top of the table was a large, messy pile. They couldn't make out what it was.

They inched closer, still holding hands, and walked into the open space. It was a room, a big circle. In the center was the table and all around the perimeter of the circle were prison cells, each one closed off with thick bars. Hanging above the wooden table were knives, saws, and metal hooks, some stained with red. A dark liquid dripped off the teeth of one of the saws, down onto the pile on the table. The moan continued, coming from a cell to the far left, out of Sophia and Samantha's eye line.

They looked at the table and the pile on top came into focus. The bottom of a torso, flesh hanging down and intestines soaked in blood bulging out all in a puddle of its own filth. The sour yet sweet smell traveled into their nose, down their throats, and mixed with whatever food was in their stomach from earlier. Samantha gasped and turned around, holding her stomach, and leaned over to vomit. She watched as Penelope's carrot soup shot out of her mouth, orange chunks hitting the floor, and that's when she saw it— a wet, slimy patch of hair. It was the scalped head of Jody, a fleshy and bloody head of hair lying in the dirt, remnants of brain matter acted as a glue for the dirt on the ground. Samantha screamed and ran back the way they came, away from the hell they discovered.

"Samantha," Sophia called and ran after her.

Samantha ran down the corridor back into the darkness, streams of tears ran down her face and snot dripped down her nose and over her upper lip. She tripped and hit the ground, losing all the energy and sanity to stand up. She didn't move. She lay there and cried on the corridor floor.

When Sophia got to her, she kneeled and helped her sit up.

"We're going to die down here," Samantha said, barely able to get words out.

As they sat on the ground, Sophia wrapped her arms around Samantha, placing Samantha's head onto her chest.

"Samantha, I know this is scary. This is where we are, and we cannot change that. We can only fight to survive. I came here knowing the dangers involved. I came here to save you. We can only be free if we fight this. You are going to see things that cannot be unseen. Things that live in your worst nightmares, but this is real. We need to get up and go back. Someone in there needs our help."

Samantha's body trembled against Sophia's chest as she silently cried tears of regret. Tears of confusion and tears of what was to come.

"I just want to go home," Samantha said, "I miss my mom."

She broke out into sobs and Officer Rey patiently sat, holding Samantha, imagining she was holding her sister Charlotte. They sat there for a couple of minutes, the only sounds that broke the silence were Samantha's panting and sniffles and the faint moaning sounds of whoever was locked in that dungeon.

"We have to get up now," Sophia said, a gentle inflection that interrupted this nightmare just for a second, enough to get Samantha to stand up.

Samantha wiped her face using her forearm.

"I'm sorry, I -" Samantha began to say.

"Don't be. You're just a kid," Sophia said, "I need to call for backup."

Samantha handed Officer Rey the phone. They walked back to the dungeon at a fast pace and stopped near the open entrance, just feet away from the wooden table in the center. Sophia texted Detective Salvino:

OPCLT come now found dungeon dead body, i have Sam

Salvino responded: OTW

Samantha stared at the wooden table up ahead and her eyes were wide, incapable of blinking.

"We need to find out who is locked in there," Sophia said, "We have to walk by that table. Hold my hand and look at me, nothing else."

They walked toward the table and Samantha stared at Sophia's dark hair but her mind kept seeing a pile of wet intestines covered in blood. Jody's hair lying on the floor detached from her head and cut along her brain, orange carrot stew vomit on the floor. She closed her eyes and forced her lips shut to keep her own vomit down.

The groaning grew louder. It was the sound of someone crying without tears and in unbearable pain.

Sophia stopped walking and Samantha opened her eyes. They were looking into a cell, and past the bars, a man sat back against the wall on the dirt floor. His right leg had been cut off at the knee and a dark, red stained sheet was wrapped tightly over it. He cried and groaned from the pain. Next to him was another person, hunched over with no sign of sound or movement. Samantha walked up to the bars and gripped them with her hands. She peered between two bars and said, "Miles?"

He sat there, shirtless and full of dirt and grime; dry blood was streaked across his body. He had a dazed look in his eyes, full of defeat. He began to move his mouth but struggled, wincing at the pain in his leg and gripping his right thigh. He closed his eyes for a while and then opened them. He moved his chapped, rough lips and said, "I...I...Ivy?"

Samantha's eyes scanned the body next to Miles and she could make out a faded jean vest, the sleeves ripped. Spiked hair and the boney carcass of old punk rock memories. A dry, dark red puddle swallowed the body into the depths of the hell they were living in.

Samantha gripped the cell bars, the veins in her knuckles bulged and screamed out as she said, "Steve? Steve! Steve! No! Steve!"

She shook the bars with the little energy she had left and then pushed her face against the bars with the hope that she'd squeeze through. With the hope of holding him in her arms one last time.

In almost a whisper, Miles said, "He's gone. He loved you and came for you."

Samantha began to cry. "He came here for me? And look at you. I'm so sorry Miles."

Sophia pulled Samantha off the bars and into her chest, wrapping her arms all the way around her. Placing her hand on

Samantha's head, Samantha's body jerked in silence as her sobs were muffled from Sophia's embrace.

With Samantha in her arms, she said, "Miles, I'm Officer Sophia Rey and I'm going to get you out of here."

Miles opened his mouth to speak but instead grabbed onto his leg again. He shook his head and his eyes were sullen. Sophia took out the key that unlocked the Red Room door in the hopes that it might work to open Miles' cell. It didn't.

"Don't worry Miles," Officer Rey said. "Help is on the way."

Miles shook his head again. He lifted his head up as he held his left leg and finally got one word out, "Run."

CHAPTER FORTY-NINE

Penelope walked into the living room where all the Freedom House members slept. They lay on the floor, shoulder to shoulder, head to feet, like sardines packed into a small, confined space. She walked over to them, placing her feet in between each body, feeling for the floor on each step she took. She found Skye and shook her awake.

"Skye. Wake up," Penelope said.

Skye opened her eyes, then her mouth widely as a yawn escaped.

"What's going on?" Skye asked.

"We have a big problem. Cyrus and Jonas are in the Red Room. Ivy and Rey are missing. Ivy lied and she stole my key."

Skye sat up, now wide awake with full attention on Penelope.

"What does Cyrus want us to do?" Skye asked.

"We need to wake up everyone. We need all of Freedom House," said Penelope.

Skye stood up and she and Penelope began waking the others.

"Wake up. Cyrus' orders," Penelope said.

All the members sat up. Penelope and Skye sat back-to-back in the middle of the living room, looking over the circle of members sitting around them.

"The Darkness is here," Penelope said.

There were confused gasps, and everyone began talking at once.

Skye raised her voice over the chatter, "We must stay calm. We have to fight the Darkness. Cyrus and Jonas went down to the Red Room and we must wait for them to return."

"Skye is right. Whether we like it or not, it's time now. Cyrus wants us to be free," Penelope said.

One of the members shouted, "Cyrus wants us free."

The sun was starting to rise and bright pink and yellow creeped through the clouds. One person after another began to chant, "Cyrus wants us free. Cyrus wants us free."

Officer Rey looked around for something, anything she could use to pick the lock to free Miles. She walked around to all the other cells. There were six total that made up the circular perimeter of the dungeon.

"Samantha, I need your help. Look for anything that might help us pick that lock."

Samantha nodded and wiped her eyes. Officer Rey walked to the prison cell next to Miles'. She picked up the lock in her hand and looked up through the bars. Inside the cell was a wooden bench against the right wall. It smelled of shit and piss. What was left of

Jody lay in the back-left corner. The inside of her brain was exposed, and flesh hung down on the sides of her head. Brain matter spilled out onto the floor where maggots systematically crawled all over it.

Officer Rey swallowed hard. The next cell was unlocked and opened a few inches.

"There's nothing here. We're not going to get Miles out," Samantha said as she held back from breaking down into a sob of tears.

"Keep looking Samantha," Officer Rey said, her fear masked with a forced calmness but, like radio waves in the air, was present all around them and inside them.

Officer Rey opened the cell door and its squeak echoed in the dungeon. Samantha stopped, looked at the detective, and walked over to the cell. She stood behind Officer Rey. Sophia walked into the cell, and like the one that swallowed Jody, it smelled of feces. Sophia lifted her right arm to her nose to block the strong scent. She walked closer to the large pile on the floor. The cell was dark, and she heard the buzzing sound of flies. There were two bodies laid out next to each other, two adult men with their stomachs cut open and intestines spilling onto the ground. Officer Rey, still with her arm to her nose, shook her head slowly back and forth.

Samantha turned around and looked back at the dungeon entrance at the dark archway, "Sophia, did you hear that?"

Officer Rey lifted her head and turned around, holding her breath to help her pinpoint any sounds. She did hear something. Someone was coming.

CHAPTER FIFTY

Officer Rey pulled Samantha down onto the ground behind the large, wooden table that lay in the center of the prison cells.

She placed her hands onto Samantha's shoulders, "Listen to me. You need to do exactly what I tell you. Do you understand?"

Tears streamed down Samantha's cheeks and fell onto her legs. She nodded but didn't speak.

"I am going to hide you, but I need you to be strong," Officer Rey said.

She pulled Samantha into the open prison cell. They stood over the two dead bodies. Samantha put her right hand over her mouth and placed her left hand over it to force herself to not make a sound.

"I need you to be strong Samantha. And no matter what you hear, do not come out. You are going to hide under these bodies. Can you do that?" Officer Rey asked.

Samantha responded in a low voice, her initial shock almost silenced her and robbed her of words, "Yes."

Sophia turned her head to see the dungeon entrance. They had to move fast. With Officer Rey on one side and Samantha on the other, they lifted the body with all the strength they had left in them and rolled it over.

"I need you to lie down," said Officer Rey.

Samantha got down onto the floor, even though it was full of dirt, grime, blood, and other chunks of human something that looked like they came out of a meat grinder. When she lied down, her back sank into the wet mess around her and pieces of flesh and intestine rubbed into her skin. Officer Rey pulled one of the corpse's shoulders to roll the body halfway onto Samantha's, a whole new meaning to the game hide and seek.

Samantha made a gasping sound and couldn't help the steady stream of tears that ran down her face and rolled onto the remains of long-gone peers of Freedom House.

"Just focus on your breathing and close your eyes. You can do this," Officer Rey said.

Samantha closed her eyes and turned her head to face the prison wall, but at least she had company lying with her. Officer Rey rolled the second corpse onto Samantha to create a casual, or organic, maybe even natural pile of death. Just a normal layout of internal organs spilling out and just the right amount of sporadic placement of limbs to not bring attention to the mound of lifelessness that Samantha used as a blanket of survival.

"It's going to be okay," Officer Rey said, and then she walked out of the prison cell, closing the cell door but leaving a small gap of open space. Samantha heard the door squeak and opened her eyes for a second; the prison wall came into her view then she shut her eyes tightly.

Officer Rey approached the wooden table, which was the home to another unfortunate Freedom House soul. Above the table there hung many different tools: knives, handsaws, and cleavers. She unhooked a knife and got down onto the floor, behind the table, and stared at the corridor entrance. She could hear something getting closer. She watched the dark entrance way and gripped the knife.

Cyrus and Jonas appeared at the entrance. Cyrus stopped and placed his hand up to signal Jonas to stop. They said nothing. Cyrus looked around the dungeon by only moving his head from left to center to the right. His eyes moved from the corpse lying on the table up to the tools hanging directly above. He walked to the first prison cell to the left and stood in front of the cell door.

"How we doing today, Miles?" he asked with a meditative smile.

Miles didn't look up. His head hung down over his chest. Cyrus walked over to the open cell. He swung the cell door open. Samantha held her breath. She could feel maggots crawling over her left shoulder as they swarmed the rotten meat that lay on top of her, the rapid movement of insects at work together: feeding, feeding, feeding. She closed her eyes and sweat built up around her hairline. She had an itch on her cheek, the kind that seemed to force your hand to reflex and move on its own, only this time she had to fight the reflex. The image of Slim Steve's rotting, bloody body flashed through her mind. That first time he offered her his cigarette, smoke curling out of his mouth, a quiet memory of his smile. With no way to wipe them away, tears ran down her face, soaking her cheeks. She could hear Cyrus' heavy feet on the floor just feet away from her and getting closer.

Samantha heard Officer Rey.

"Looking for something?" Officer Rey asked.

Cyrus turned around still standing inside the open prison cell. Officer Rey was next to the wood table and holding a knife to Jonas' throat. Cyrus' expression remained unmoved.

"It's over. Freedom House is over," Officer Rey said as she had one arm wrapped around Jonas' neck, the knife pressed against his skin. Her hand shook while her eyes stayed locked into Cyrus'. Jonas tried to see his neck with his eyes, thinking if he could only get a glimpse then all of this would somehow stop, and he'd be awakened from this nightmare.

Cyrus said, "It's never over Officer Rey. I know why you're here but you have no fucking clue why I'm here. "It's over," Sophia said as her eyes widened at the sound of her name coming out of his mouth.

"You lost something long ago. Something dear to your heart and it was your fault. You haven't forgiven yourself and you never will. A piece of you has been lost with it. Isn't that right? "

"You don't know what you're talking about," Sophia said.

"Officer, I beg to differ. It's you who doesn't know."

Walking out of the prison cell, Cyrus walked toward Officer Rey and Jonas. He took his time. Each step moved with a purpose.

"I was once told that I would reach the kingdom, where all truth was waiting for me. The problem is that not all of us want to reach something. We'd rather convince others it exists and then destroy them while they seek their kingdom, their light. I am a destroyer Sophia."

"You're referring to the Kingdom of Light?" Sophia said.

"You are smart but unfortunately your timing and intelligence are out of sync. And timing is everything. Kingdom of Light's leader, Apollo, believed in a kingdom. I was there when he took his life along with the rest of them. I saw the power Apollo had over them and I knew what I had to do."

"This? Your Journey to Freedom? You're sick and need help."

"You still don't get it. I am not like Apollo. He believed in the light with his followers. I believe in destroying mine. People search their entire lives for someone to tell them of their importance, to show them the meaning of life, when it's right there in front of them, but they're too weak to figure it out. The sheep of our existence. Isn't that right Jonas?"

"I understand Cyrus. Destroying us will bring truth to the world," Jonas said.

"Jonas, he wants to kill you all for nothing," Sophia said.

"Your words mean nothing here. Now, where is Ivy?" Cyrus asked and he continued to walk toward Sophia.

"I came down here to look for her," Sophia said.

She backed herself up against one of the prison cell doors as Cyrus walked up to her with the same steady speed, a walking chase that made her palms sweaty. She gripped the knife against Jonas, but the clammy residue of her palms played a game of slip and slide between her hand and the knife handle.

Cyrus stopped only a couple of feet away from Jonas.

"My Jonas. Such a loyal and intelligent soul." Cyrus stood with his hands resting against his lower back as if standing in a park and admiring a willow. The beauty of its weeping, tendril-like branches and leaves, but always with that underlying sadness, as its branches frown down to touch the ground.

Officer Rey held Jonas' head back and tried to grip the knife steadily amongst the slime of sweat, the slime of fear, that seeped out of her palms. She stared at Cyrus and although her eyes never left his, her mind was time traveling into the past and back to the day that she lost Charlotte. The song of the ice cream truck, like that of a jewelry box chime, echoed through the neighborhood. It got closer and Charlotte turned around. She didn't have enough coins. *We could've gone straight home. I gave her enough to get an ice cream and she didn't even get her ice cream. I gave her enough.*

"Thinking about what you lost Rey?" Cyrus asked, his hands still resting behind him with a gentle ease.

"It's over now. It's time to end this," Officer Rey said.

"You're right. I knew The Darkness was coming, and now, it's here," Cyrus smiled.

He reached up and cupped Jonas' cheek in his hand. He touched it with the care and love of a father to a son and looked into Jonas' eyes and whispered, "It's your time to be free now."

Cyrus kept his right hand on Jonas' cheek and with his left hand he grabbed Officer Rey's wrist and used her hand as his own. He pushed the detective's hand into Jonas' throat, and as the knife sliced into his neck, his skin split open and blood began to trickle down his chest. Jonas' eyes widened, but he resisted a fight because he knew it was time to be free.

"Noooooo!" Officer Rey screamed.

Jonas reached his arms out to Cyrus, and Cyrus wrapped his arms around Jonas, allowing his body weight to fully submerge onto him. He hugged him and went onto his knees, bringing Jonas onto the ground. Warm blood spread between both of their chests. Cyrus laid Jonas down and he stood up. Officer Rey held the knife, but her hand shook in small intervals back and forth.

"What have you done?" Cyrus asked.

"I...I didn-," Officer Rey dropped the knife. Tears fell down her face and she shook her head in a repetitive motion. Cyrus moved at the same calm pace as before. He leaned over and picked up the knife. Officer Rey stared at Jonas' dead body on the floor and she cupped her mouth with her hand and cried, trying to hold the sounds in and tuck them far down into the depths of her stomach.

Cyrus held the knife down to his side with no attempt to hide it.

"Rey, don't you want to be set free of all of this? The Darkness from your past doesn't need to dictate your future," Cyrus said as he used his left, bare hand to wipe Jonas' blood off the knife.

He raised his left hand to his nose and smelled it the way someone smells a vanilla peach candle.

"You're sick. I can help you," Officer Rey's voice cracked with fear but was spoken with hope.

"It's time for you to be free," Cyrus said.

That's when Samantha crawled out from under the mound of flesh and squirming maggots, stood up, and said, "Cyrus, weren't you looking for me?"

CHAPTER FIFTY-ONE

Detective Salvino raced down the 1 North with his sirens blaring. He thought about the house in Boulder Creek. He heard the twisting sound of all the ropes hanging from the ceiling and all the naked bodies in multiple rows, a grid and pattern of the lost souls that just needed some guidance. He thought of the girl who hung there with her bulging eyes and veins ready to pop out of her neck and jaw. He saw her, hanging there with her head slumped down and her shoulders pulsating from her giggles. She laughed at him.

Police cars followed right behind Salvino. He got to the turn and gunned it around the corner. The road was bumpy and uneven. Tall redwood trees towered over and passed by his window as red brown blurs of brushstrokes. He drove up and slammed on his brakes, bringing the car to an angle to give him cover from whatever bullshit was about to arise.

He opened the car door. As he stepped out of the car, he stayed facing toward Freedom House and its commune garden. A healthy dosage of vegetables sprinkled the front of the house. Tomato plants, corn, and carrots stood between the police cars and the entrance to Freedom House. Detective Salvino got onto his right knee and kept his left foot up at a ninety-degree angle. He stayed behind the car door and took his gun out, pointing it out the window frame of the car door toward the house. As police cars rolled up behind him, they positioned themselves in the same strategic line up.

Inside of Freedom House, the members were still sitting and waiting for Cyrus. Penelope and Skye sat in the center with everyone else sitting around them. When they heard the police sirens, some of them gasped and turned their heads to the front door.

"It's okay," Penelope said. "The Darkness is here. Cyrus knew it and he warned us. We must free ourselves from it. We cannot surrender to The Outside. We've worked too hard for our freedom."

Someone asked, "What should we do? Cyrus isn't back yet."

"We will do what we know Cyrus wants. We must begin the Journey to Freedom," Skye said.

Skye stood up and walked down the hallway and into the Yoga Room. She returned with two large canisters of gas.

"We finally get to complete our journey," Skye said.

She looked around at all the Freedom House members sitting in the living room. The twinkle and gloss over their eyes confirmed that they were ready to be set free. They had been waiting for this and working for it for a long time.

"Just sit and wait," Skye said.

She started in the living room, pouring the gasoline along the perimeter of the walls. Then she moved into the kitchen. She held the gas can with two hands and spilled the gas onto the kitchen floor tiles.

"We should hold hands," Penelope said, the thrill of all this was apparent in the excitement in her voice. Everyone grabbed the hand of the person to their right and to their left.

"Let's meditate. Close your eyes and inhale deeply into your stomach. Now exhale slowly. Continue to focus on your breath. Each breath is getting us closer to freedom, to enlightenment." Penelope spoke slow and steady with a calmness. Skye walked out of the kitchen, through the living room, and into the hallway. She put down the empty gas can and picked up a full one. She splashed the hallway walls and blessed each room with the propane liquid. She got to the end of the hallway and stopped. She stared at the red door that stared back at her.

She whispered, "We'll see you on the other side Cyrus." Then, she threw gas onto the red door.

CHAPTER FIFTY-TWO

Samantha stood up from under the bodies, her smooth skin was covered in human slush and dirt. She walked out of the dungeon cell. If he was shocked, he didn't show it at all. Cyrus smiled a genuine smile like he was seeing a good friend that he hadn't seen in ages.

"Ivy, yes. I was looking for you. And now you have been found."

"Samantha, come with me," Officer Rey said, loud and clear without hesitation.

Cyrus walked up to Samantha at the pace of a priest ready to deliver a sermon.

He caressed the bottom of her chin with his thumb and said, "Your name is Ivy and I promised you freedom. I promised you enlightenment."

Samantha yanked her head away, but she kept her eyes on his face.

Officer Rey began to move toward them. Cyrus raised his hand eye level, index finger raised, and made the sound, "Ah," signaling Sophia to think again.

"You came all this way Sophia. You wouldn't want to make another mistake, would you? Another loss to live with?" Cyrus looked at Officer Rey as he spoke.

"You feed off the weak. That's the only power you have. The weak and the young," Sophia said.

"Wrong answer." Cyrus grabbed Samantha's shoulder and pulled her into him. He shoved the knife into her lower stomach and cut upward, above her belly button, eviscerating all her hopes and dreams. Samantha leaned on Cyrus and he pulled the knife out, holding it in his right hand. He used his right hand to hug her head and hold the knife and he kissed the top of her head.

"I promised you, Ivy," Cyrus said. "Now you can be free."

Officer Rey fell to her knees, her mouth wide open, but no sound came out. Everything went silent for her in that moment, just a replay on mute. Cyrus walked backward with his eyes on Officer Rey and watched her as she stared at Samantha Leslie Watson, age fourteen, brown hair and brown eyes.

Walking backward to the corridor entrance, he stood there looking down at Officer Rey. "You could've been free too. Living through this will just add to your nightmares," he said, then turned the corner and was gone.

Officer Rey was still on her knees and crawled to Samantha's body. She lifted Samantha onto her lap and sat on the floor rocking her back and forth. Sophia hid her face in the crevice of Samantha's neck and screamed as loud as she could. She lifted her head up, and lying in her arms for a brief second, was her sister Charlotte.

Charlotte's neck had dark purple ligature marks and the veins in her eyes had popped. Charlotte lifted her head up with full speed and wrapped her hands around Officer Rey's neck. Her strength was not that of a young girl. Sophia tried to pull Charlotte's hands off, but it was a futile attempt.

"See what they did to me Soph. You see what they did. Why did you give me a quarter and a dime for an ice cream? Look what they did to me. A quarter and a dime, a real nice time. A quarter and a dime, a real nice time," she shouted, and the inside of her mouth was caked with black, oozing liquid.

Officer Rey broke free and ran. She turned to look back. It was no longer Charlotte. It was Samantha, her insides flopped out of her stomach and onto the ground. Samantha was shouting, "A quarter and a dime, a real nice time. A quarter and a dime, a real nice time."

Sophia ran back into the darkness of the corridor, and out of the dungeon as fast as she could.

CHAPTER FIFTY-THREE

Skye and Penelope sat in the center and everyone else sat in a circle around them. Outside they heard Detective Salvino speak over the police car loudspeaker:

"Come out with your hands up. That's a direct order. Everyone come out with hands up."

Inside, they all sat as if they heard nothing. Skye took the gas can and poured some on her arms and rubbed it into her skin like lotion. She passed it to Penelope. Penelope rubbed the gas on her chest and up her neck in a massaging motion. The other members scooted closer and held out their arms. They rubbed gas on each other and giggled playfully.

The loudspeaker again:

"Come out with your hands up. Everyone out with hands up. We will be forced to move in if you do not follow orders."

Penelope stood up and skipped to the kitchen. She opened the drawer next to the stove, took out a matchbox, and skipped back to the living room and sat down. From the hallway, Cyrus walked into the living room.

"Cyrus. You made it," Penelope said.

"I wouldn't miss it. The Darkness is here. We must set ourselves free and together join the light. I have one more special gift for you all. It's in my room out back. I will bring it to you. But you must begin the Journey to Freedom. I'll meet you there when I return with your gift." Cyrus smiled. As the members sat on the floor, he walked around and touched their heads. They hugged his legs.

"We'll meet you there," Penelope said, "We'll meet you there."

All the members said it together. "We'll meet you there. We'll meet you there. We'll meet you there."

Loudspeaker:

"This is your last warning. Come out with your hands up."

Cyrus turned around and walked to the kitchen. Penelope watched him and knew she'd see him soon. He walked out of Freedom House and into Freedom Park. And just like that, he was gone.

They all continued to chant, "We'll meet you there. We'll meet you there."

Penelope lit the match and in one second, the crisp sound of flame filled the air. Penelope's face was bright from the match as she held it and stared into it. Then she dropped it onto her lap. The flame that started out as an infant, the flame that could've been put out with a thumb and index finger, hit the carpet between her legs and crawled across the floor in all directions. In seconds, it scattered over the living room, immersing all the Freedom House souls within its grip. No one got up. No one ran. And no one screamed.

Within the clouded smoke and bright yellow flames, the people of Freedom House melted into their skin and turned black like tar. They held hands but their flesh peeled off into each other's palms. The flames split into two paths, one to the kitchen and one down the hallway. The front windows of the house shattered out with a loud cracking and the cloud of smoke and blinding flames pushed out and hugged the outside walls of Freedom House.

Detective Salvino and the officers ducked down behind their vehicles and covered their heads.

"You've got to be fucking kidding me," Detective Salvino said.

He grabbed his radio: This is Detective Salvino. We need the fire department here five minutes ago. 1648 Mill Road off the 1. Officer down and kids inside. Over."

A voice immediately replied, "Confirmed. Fire department on their way."

The flames multiplied and climbed higher and higher. Detective Salvino shouted over the sound of the angry flames, ripping and roaring out of control. "Officer Rey is inside. I'm going around the back to see if there's a way in. Fire department is on their way."

Detective Salvino held his gun with both hands. He moved fast and went around the left side of the house. A small stone path led into Freedom Park; the animals were to the left. The chickens were running frantically in their cage. The heat overwhelmed his skin and he had to move back, away from the house. Whatever was inside had no chance. Any attempt to go inside would be a free ride to death. *Train will be leaving in five minutes. Hop on the Death Express.*

He went back the way he came and walked out to the front. Police cars surrounded the house and officers watched without any way to help. Fire trucks came wailing up, sirens screaming over the rumbling fire. Firemen jumped out of the truck and executed each action, every moment, with swift precision. They communicated with their eyes and each one had a particular set of tasks assigned.

They moved fast. In less than a minute they were trying to get the fire under control.

The one in charge walked up to Detective Salvino, "Detective. Heard there's an officer inside, that correct?"

Detective Salvino stared at the house with a mix of anger and worry, "Correct."

The fireman left Detective Salvino alone and went over to a group of firemen huddled together and began giving directions. They were nodding their heads, and then four of them walked to the front door, broke it down, and disappeared inside the house.

Detective Salvino watched as thick, heavy water shot out of the hoses and crashed against the black smoke and slithering flames. He watched as they battled the flames even though the fire had won, and they all knew it. He stood there, and just watched.

CHAPTER FIFTY-FOUR

Officer Rey ran down the pitch-black corridor, holding onto the cold cement walls with her palms. She could hear Samantha's voice growing farther away. *A quarter and a dime, a real nice time.* She hugged the wall and continued to run back to the red door. *Samantha was dead, but she was talking, and she knew about Charlotte and the coins.*

In the distance, Officer Rey saw a faint light creeping around a corner. She was getting closer to her destination. She ran to the light and turned the corner. She knew she wasn't far from the red door. She ran as fast as she could and gradually slowed down when she smelled something burning. She slowed to a cautious and hesitant walk until she stood at the bottom of the cement stairs that led up to the red door. She looked up the stairs and watched as smoke creeped through the bottom crack and up into the air. Lifting her arm to her nose, she squinted her dark almond eyes and walked up the stairs. She used her left fingers to jab at the doorknob, full of certainty that the doorknob would be too hot to touch.

She stared at the red door and the fast-paced thoughts of nothing and everything all at once scrambled around in her mind. She had no way out and no solution to this. She turned back and looked down the cement stairs. She could only go back to the darkness that haunted her and the death that waited for her down there. The smoke was coming in faster and filling the top of the stairs. Officer Rey looked at the red door one last time and walked back down the stairs. She got to the bottom and faced the corridor with only the dimness of flickering lights keeping her company.

CHAPTER FIFTY-FIVE

Like a broken record, she was walking down the corridor again, back to the dungeon. The rats squeaked at her feet and ran in the same direction she was going. The lights flickered and then went out and she was standing in darkness once again. A sound emerged from the blackness that surrounded her; the low sound of music in the distance. It sounded like the chime of a music box. It grew closer and louder. It wasn't a music box. It was the music of an ice cream truck. She stopped and pushed her back against the wall covering her ears with her hands.

She could hear the muffled sounds of carnival music as it grew louder. She pushed her hands into her ears with full force and closed her eyes. Then silence. It stopped. She opened her eyes and moved her hands off her ears with caution. Nothing.

She heard another noise. Something light against the floor, like air blowing across the ground. She felt a swift breeze pass around her. The darkness made it difficult to see anything but then she realized. Someone was riding a bike past her, back and forth.

Sophia whispered, "Charlotte?"

A voice pierced through the dark, "A quarter and a dime, a real nice time. Why did you give me money for ice cream? He showed me a real nice time. He did again, and again, and again."

It's in my head. It's in my head. Just breathe, breathe. Fuck. Officer Rey slid down the wall and sat on the ground, hugging her knees to her stomach. She covered her ears and tucked her head into her legs. *Stop, please stop.* The darkness swallowed her. She was alone with her thoughts and alone with death. Time disappeared for her, the way it does in dreams and especially in nightmares. Time was static and stuck in one continuous loop of terror.

CHAPTER FIFTY-SIX

Sophia wasn't sure when she snapped out of it. She heard a muffled voice, the type of sounds you hear when under water. It was coming into clarity, that moment you look up to the water's surface, swim toward it, and break free into the air.

A fireman was saying her name: "Officer Rey, Sophia Rey? Nod your head if you hear my voice. Officer, nod your head if you hear my voice."

With her head still down in her knees, Sophia opened her eyes. The voice became crisp and clear. She lifted her head up slowly and with her best attempt, tried to nod. A flashlight was pointing to the floor at her feet. She looked down the long corridor, but nothing was there.

"Whe...where...where's Charlotte?" Officer Rey asked.

"Officer? You're going to be okay. Let's get you out of here."

"She's dead. She's dead," Officer Rey said in a monotone whisper.

"Who?"

"Samantha. She's down there." Officer Rey turned her head and pointed down the corridor.

"Let's get you out of here," the fireman looked at the other two firemen, "Need a check down there."

The firemen moved fast and started down the corridor. They flashed their lights along the corridor walls and jagged, sharp shadows danced down to the dungeon.

"Wrap your arms around my neck. I'll help you up."

Sophia put her arms around the fireman, his thick yellow jacket and broad shoulders were comforting. He lifted her up with him and she hugged him harder, laying her face onto his shoulder. She let out defeated tears and he welcomed it.

He patted her on the back, "It's going to be okay."

She lifted her head, wiped her face, and kept one arm around his neck. He put his arm around her waist to hold her up as they turned their backs to the dark. They walked up the cement stairs and through what used to be the red door. There was nothing left of Freedom House except burnt remains of a house once lived in with the ash of human flesh and bones mixed in. Sophia looked around,

"Was he in here?" she asked the fireman.

"Who?"

"Cyrus," Sophia said.

"I don't know. I'm going to pick you up and carry you out of this mess, okay?"

She gave a slow nod. The walls were stripped to skeleton frames with piles of wood, broken appliances, and deteriorated furniture in mounds across the floor. The back wall was gone and when standing inside what used to be the living room, Freedom Park could be seen through the remnants of the kitchen. The red and blue flashing lights from the police cars out front knocked at the door of memories Officer Rey tried to keep locked away. She remembered those same lights flashing along her street when she was a little girl. She remembered Charlotte, and now Samantha.

The fireman carried her out the front doorway and she looked up at the blue sky hidden behind dark clouds of black smoke. The sound of ambulance sirens and firemen working through the rubbish were muted out as Sophia Rey stared up at the sky. Detective Salvino ran up to them.

"You okay to walk?" asked the fireman.

"Yeah."

He set her feet down first and held her arms as she stood up.

"Sophia, I'm so glad you're alive," Detective Salvino said.

"Did you find him?" Officer Rey asked.

"Not yet. It was a mass suicide." Detective Salvino stared into her eyes.

"Samantha Watson is dead. He killed her. Eviscerated her right in front of me." Officer Rey's eyes widened. "There's a survivor down there. His name is Miles. One of his legs is partially cut off. Detective, Cyrus didn't kill himself with them. We have to find him."

Sophia turned toward the house, but Salvino grabbed her arm.

"Sophia, the firemen are down there. They'll find him. We'll let paramedics know about Samantha."

But Sophia didn't care what Detective Salvino was saying. She turned around and ran back inside Freedom House.

CHAPTER FIFTY-SEVEN

She could hear Detective Salvino's feet not far behind her. As she ran through the house, remains of burnt carpet, wood, and sticky black flesh stuck to the bottom of her shoes.

"Sophia, wait," Salvino called after her.

Officer Rey got to the doorway that led down to the dungeon and with no hesitation she made her way down, past the firemen.

"Should we stop her?" one asked Salvino.

Detective Salvino brushed past the fireman and said, "No. Let her go."

Now the corridor was lit up with portable lights all the way down. Officer Rey briskly walked down the corridor without looking back. The underground tunnel that was once a lifeless void of darkness was now transformed by bright lights and the many firemen working down there. No rats, no darkness, and no more melodies echoing that of childhood ice cream memories.

Officer Rey got to the end of the corridor that opened into the wide dungeon. She could see the bright yellow jackets of two firemen who were kneeling inside of the cell that Miles was in. She peered around the wooden table that sat in the center. Her eyes scanned the ground.

"Officer Rey. We found two young men," one of the firemen said as Detective Salvino walked up.

"Miles and Steve," Sophia said, "Samantha Watson is down here too, dead."

The fireman gave a long stare before speaking. "Officer, there's no female body down here except one in that cell and that one's been here for some time. "

"That's not possible. Samantha was killed in front of me. She died right there on the floor."

"There was no dead body there when we arrived on scene."

Detective Salvino chimed in, "Sounds like we just need to look harder then. Officer Rey, why don't you head back upstairs and—"

"I'm staying right here. Samantha Watson died, and her body was right there. Maybe Miles saw something."

The two firemen stood up. "Miles is dead. We tried but he lost way too much blood."

Miles' body sat against the wall, stiff and covered in dirt and blood as if he bathed in it for days.

"The female victim is Jody. That's probably not her real name but that's what they called her," Officer Rey said, "Salvino, let's check the backyard."

They made their way back through the corridor and up the stairs. They walked out to Freedom Park and down the stone path.

"This is where their leader stayed. They called him Cyrus," Sophia said.

"He could've been in that fire Sophia," Detective Salvino said.

"Listen to me detective. He wasn't in that fire. Remember the survivor of Kingdom of Light? It was him. He survived because he never believed in it. He called himself a destroyer and he will continue on until he's stopped."

"How do you know?"

"He told me down there. This isn't over," Sophia said.

"You're right. It's never really over. It lurks everywhere, waiting to pounce. You did your best here Sophia."

"My best wasn't good enough."

They walked into the room and small, tea light candles brightened the perimeter along the walls. It was one large room and there were no doors leading anywhere else. It was quiet and desolate, and the only movement was that of the candle lights flickering around them, giggling at them as they tried to find Cyrus. There was a table at the other end of the room, where the long carpet ended. The darkness made it difficult to see but Officer Rey could make out an object underneath the table.

She walked down the carpet and when she got to the table, she bent down to see what it was. A small black safe. The safe door was cracked open.

"It's a safe. It's been opened," Officer Rey said and turned back to Detective Salvino.

"I'll get forensics over here to check for fingerprints," he said.

Officer Rey and Detective Salvino stood back as forensics pulled the safe door fully open. Whatever had been in there was long gone and had disappeared with Cyrus. They checked for fingerprints and got nothing. No traces of him were left behind except the piles of a burnt-up house once known as Freedom House.

"He's gone," Officer Rey shook her head.

"Looks like we'll be on a manhunt," Salvino said, staring down at the safe.

CHAPTER FIFTY-EIGHT

Helicopters flew overhead, high above the trees, and the patterned sounds of their blades violently whirled through the air. It was about 6:00 a.m. The meadow field that spanned miles in front of Freedom House swayed from the light breeze. Just past the meadow, the redwoods stood tall, always watching over.

Freedom House was nothing but black, smoked walls and skeletal frames of a house that once stood. Piles of jagged, long pieces of wood stuck out from the ground. Officer Rey sat in the back of the ambulance, her legs hanging down off the edge as she stared at what remained. In her peripheral, she saw something white running near the back of the house, near Freedom Park. It was the white peacock running into the meadow, its long white feathers wisped in the wind as it ran towards the redwoods.

Detective Salvino walked up to the ambulance. "You okay Sophia?"

"I will be," she said.

"We're going to keep looking until we're exhausted. Then, we're going to look some more," Detective Salvino said, placing his hand onto her shoulder.

She was quiet.

"Officer Rey, it's not your fault," Salvino said.

Officer Rey's eyes hardened at the brow, "Then whose?"

"I've been doing this for some time now. I've come to accept that sometimes, there's no explanation. There exists pure darkness in some people. A darkness so pure, explanation is non-existent. An evil that exists just for the sake of evil."

Detective Salvino turned around and walked to his car. He stopped and looked back, "Officer Rey. Take some time off. Get some rest."

She nodded her head at him, and he turned around and got into his car. She watched as he drove off. She listened to the helicopters overhead as they searched for something that no one really knew anything about. They searched until they were exhausted. Then they searched some more.

They never found Cyrus. They never found Samantha Watson. They only found another scene just like the Boulder Creek one. One that would add to their nightmares for the rest of their lives. Officer Rey couldn't save Charlotte and she couldn't save Samantha. The ice cream truck song, Charlotte's bike on the ground, the dark figure in the truck who took her sister, Samantha's eviscerated missing body— it all raced through her mind. She closed her eyes and opened them, snapping herself out of her own thoughts.

As she sat in the back of the ambulance, she looked at the burnt remains of Freedom House. The roof was now just a blackened skeleton, flesh melted away as piles of ash on the ground. The members of Freedom House were in the air around her as smoke residue, seeping into her eyes and mouth, suffocating her. Gasping for air, Sophia Rey knew she would never be set free until she found Cyrus and vindicated the dead. But first, she needed to return home to lay Charlotte to rest.

About the Author

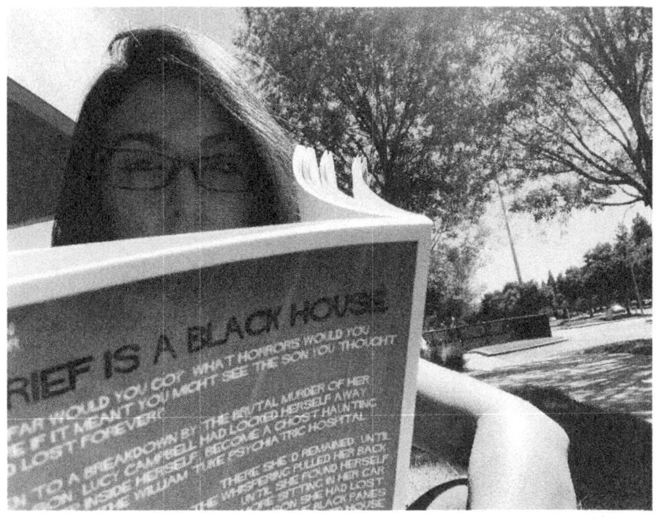

Stephanie Evelyn writes short stories and novels that span across horror, suspense, and thriller genres. She has a bachelor's degree in Film and Digital Media and is also a painter. She goes by the nickname Sterp.

iamsterp.com

Made in the USA
Las Vegas, NV
01 October 2024